VICTORY FOR VAMPIRES

A HAVEN EVER AFTER NOVELLA

HAZEL MACK

COPYRIGHT

© Hazel Mack Author 2024

EBook ISBN: 978-1-957873-78-7

Paperback ISBN: 978-1-957873-58-9

All rights reserved. No part of this publication may be reproduced, stored or transmitted in any form or by any means, electronic, mechanical, photocopying, recording, scanning, or otherwise without written permission from the publisher. It is illegal to copy this book, post it to a website, or distribute it by any other means without permission.

This novel is entirely a work of fiction. The names, characters and incidents portrayed in it are the work of the author's imagination. Any resemblance to actual persons, living or dead, events or localities is entirely coincidental. However, if I get the chance to become Ever's newest resident, I'll take it!

I don't support the use of AI in book, book cover or book graphic creation. I do not authorize the uploading of or learning from any of my books into an AI. If you love human generated books, please feel free to learn more at my website here: www.annafury.com/ai

Cover - Anna Fury Author

Cover Art - Linda Noeran (@linda.noeran)

❀ Created with Vellum

1

VALENTINA

"Valentina, what do you think?"

My boss's question pulls my focus from the snow falling outside the meeting room window. Thankfully, I was prepared for this meeting.

Evenia stands at the opposite end of the black burled meeting table, both palms flat on the surface. One forefinger taps quickly on the wood, a sure sign she's irritated. But, of all the planners on our haven planning team, I truly believe I'm the only one she likes.

I sigh. "Well, I've dug deep into every haven assessment we've done on Azuro. There's no good way to expand without getting close to the human town there, which is already planning a large expansion over the next ten years. Nothing nearby is ideal. The expense to try expanding that haven is actually *greater* than starting from scratch with a new haven. So—" I glance around the room at my coworkers, "—my vote is that we move forward with a second haven, ideally on the southern end of the Italian boot."

Nobody says a word. Evenia straightens, crossing her arms as she glances around the room at the other six designers on my team.

"Well?" Her question snaps through the room like lightning. I know for a fact at least five of the six are utterly terrified of our leader.

She lets out a displeased-sounding growl. "Does nobody have a single thought on this project?"

Razeri, another vampire, sits up straight and runs one hand through his pitch-black hair. "I agree with Valentina. We've poured over the potential plans for Azuro's expansion, but it will be incredibly expensive and difficult."

I smirk. Way to say exactly what I just said.

As the rest of the team scrambles to find something new and interesting to share, I look at Evenia, letting my smile widen.

"We need a new haven, Boss." I know she can hear me down the long table. "And I want to be the one to design it."

It would be my first full haven project, something for which I've been laying the groundwork for a long time. But if I can get this right, I can ask her for a promotion I've wanted my whole life: Chief Haven Designer. Technically, she holds that title now, only because she doesn't trust anyone else to do it.

But I can do it. I'm confident of that.

The room falls silent, my coworkers sitting back in their chairs as Evenia smiles at me. She's a snake—we all know it. But she's relentlessly dedicated to the success of the haven system, and so I, too, am relentlessly dedicated to it.

"Done," Evenia barks.

Razeri startles in his seat.

I resist the urge to roll my eyes.

"Get out," Evenia commands.

We all know she's talking about everybody but me. So, I stay while the other six file out of the dark, elegant meeting room. She doesn't watch them go, but when we're alone in the room, she rounds the table and stalks to my side. Black nails thrum against her forearm as she eyes me like a viper.

"I know why you want to take on this project, Valentina," she says in a simpering, evil tone. "And I also know what's at stake if you fuck it up." She brings a black-tipped nail beneath my chin and lifts so I'm forced to stare into narrowed crimson eyes. "So don't fuck up, my little dove."

It's something she's called me since the one time she saw my shadow wings and discovered they're on the smaller side for a vampire. Little dove. It's not a complimentary nickname, but it's a nickname from the cruelest, harshest, smartest female I know. So, I'll take it.

"I won't fail." I pull my lips into a smile that matches hers. "I've never let you down yet, Evenia."

She removes her nail from my chin and spins on one elegant red-soled heel. "See that you don't," she casts over her shoulder as she disappears out of the conference room door.

When she's gone, I allow myself to slump backward in my seat. I brush my sweaty palms down my black trousers. I prepared like crazy for this meeting, but I've been in enough of them with Evenia to know they can easily go sideways. Closing my eyes, I search inward for the bond I share with Pietro, though he's far.

I can't feel him; I knew I wouldn't be able to. It never stops me searching for it, though. I wonder what he is doing right this moment? Probably making coffee with our mate, Alessandro, by his side. They adore coffee.

Our relationship is complicated. Technically, only Pietro and I share the vampiric mate bond. But Alé is just as much a part of our love despite not having that bond. It's always been the three of us. It'll always *be* the three of us.

Smiling, I think about the last time I saw them, when we stole a weekend to enjoy each other before returning to our respective havens. Their dreams and my dreams haven't aligned...yet. But vampires are some of the longer-lived monsters.

The need to see them grows stronger by the day. My wish to spend time with them becomes nearly painful by the time I pack my bag and head out of Hearth HQ's elegant black stone offices. Above me, the sky is dark and ominous, but I love it here. So different from the sun-drenched olive fields of Azuro where Pietro, Alé, and I grew up. I love that it snows here all the time, that it's dark and cold and starkly beautiful. Glancing above Dakar, the inky village built up around headquarters, I admire the jagged black mountain range that soars into an ominous sky.

Opening my mouth to catch snowflakes, I focus on their taste. The weather here is manufactured like every other haven. Snowflakes hit my tongue and dissolve. I drink them down before crossing a black cobblestone street. Heading left, I pass the bookshop and an armory. I stop at the window.

I love the armory. Inside, four gargoyles and a rock troll stand to be fitted for their weapons. The protector academy is just on the other side of the haven, so these will be upcoming graduates. Once they receive official protector status, they'll be assigned to havens all over the world to keep monsters safe from dark magic...and humanity.

Musing over that, I walk up a few more doors. When I arrive at my destination, Brion, I dip inside with a smile. My friend Ybris sits at the bar with a blood cocktail in one hand. She sips delicately at it, flirting with the bartender. Rolling my eyes, I join her when he turns from us.

Bumping her hip, I laugh and bend toward her ear. "Haven't you fucked him enough times to stop bothering with the flirting when we come here?"

Crimson eyes flash at me as she tosses her long black braid over her shoulder. "It's called edging, darling, and he loves it."

The bartender, a handsome minotaur with gorgeous long horns, blushes to the edges of his pale cheeks. The ring in his nose quivers as he stares at my friend. Oh yes, I think perhaps there's a little something more there than just sex. But relationships happen on their own time. I know that better than anyone.

Ybris slips a folded piece of paper across the bar toward the minotaur. He takes it, reads it, and runs a hand through his wavy dark hair. Tucking the note into a pocket of his vest, he wheels away from us to help another monster at the far end of the bar.

"Gods, that's going to be delicious later!" Ybris practically vibrates with excitement.

"Jealous," I huff as I steal a sip from her drink. "I miss my mates."

She gives me a sad look, then steals her drink back. "So, go visit." Her innocent look turns wicked. "Ever is one of our most successful havens. Go do some—" she makes air quotes with one hand, "—research."

I order a drink as I consider that. Ever's had its share of challenges lately with thrall attacks and the like. The magical wards that protect monster communities from the outside world are like a homing beacon for monsters turned thrall. But that's no different from most havens.

Realistically, I should probably travel to a variety of monster cities to see how they do things. Just because we did it one way in Azuro does not mean the new Italian haven needs to function in the same manner.

My drink arrives, but it's clear the bartender's focused on my friend. He jerks his head toward the back of the bar, staring at her like he can't get enough, like the only sustenance he'll ever need is her. His heated gaze sends a coil of heat through me. I have that.

Far away.

Ybris slips off her stool without looking away from him. He breaks the gaze first, heading toward the far end of the bar where he speaks quietly to the second bartender. The other male nods, grinning at the big minotaur as he claps him on the shoulder.

Ybris leaves me behind without a backward glance, disappearing down a dark hallway toward the restrooms.

Damn. We were supposed to catch up on today's meeting. But I can't begrudge my friend the sort of dalliance she's about to have. After slapping a bill on the bar top, I down my drink in a series of quick gulps. Drink devoured, I turn to leave. A dark elf by the door catches my eye, licking his lips suggestively.

Another time, I might take him up on the unspoken offer. For my kind, sex and blood are inextricably intertwined. I've taken many lovers in the time I've lived at the headquarters haven. It's natural, almost expected, that I should do so—such is vampire culture. Pietro and Alé are free to do the same, of course, and I hope they have.

Yet something stops me this time…that quiet place in my chest where I should feel my mates. Sighing, I leave the bar, ignoring the dark elf's sorrowful stare when I pay him no further attention.

Perhaps tonight, my mates are enjoying someone in the quiet, remote little haven of Ever. I hope they're having fun. I miss them terribly.

2
PIETRO

I bend to smell the enormous bouquet of flowers in my arms, straight black hair falling over my eyes. Ohken has outdone himself with today's arrangement. Blood-red roses and black dahlias are peppered with the darkest of green leaves, so dark they're nearly black. Absolutely stunning.

"Happy with your order, Pietro?" His deep voice breaks through my thoughts.

Brushing my hair back, I pull in another quick whiff before smiling up at the enormous green troll.

"Perfetto," I say with a big grin. "And the scent? Delicious, my friend. This will be beautiful on the countertop at the store." I love how the flowers match the swirling tattoos that line my neck and trail down my chest to my stomach. Not to mention, their aroma reminds me a bit of home. Well, not my home haven, specifically. They remind me of her.

Valentina.

My compliment brings a smile to Ohken's rugged face, lips splitting to reveal the short lower jaw tusks common among his kind.

Once I've paid, he strolls casually around the checkout

counter, crossing the store to pull the door open for me. I'm tall, but the flowers are so big, I can barely see over their elegant blossoms.

Clutching the base carefully, I step out of Fleur and nod my thanks to Ohken. Out on the street, new scents and noises fill my sensitive ears and nose. I twitch the pointed tip of one ear to catch conversations happening around me. It's just the usual early morning chatter from my neighbors.

Main Street is busy despite the early hour. Although, monsters keep all sorts of hours, so it's rarely completely dead on Main. Various monsters call out my name and wave hello as I cross over, walking past Miriam's Sweets and Scoops Ice Cream.

Somehow, all I seem to notice is that Main Street seems full of couples. There's the centaur pair crossing the opposite direction, smiling and waving at me. Two shifters sit on the sidewalk outside of Scoops, licking melty ice cream cones. And then, of course, a *group* of couples are leaving my coffee shop, Higher Grounds.

Couples don't usually bother me. Seeing *love* doesn't usually bother me. But lately, the age-old ache to have *someone* is more persistent. My brother, Alessandro, says it's homesickness, that I simply miss Azuro, our home haven. But I know my melancholy isn't a result of that. Home is where he and I are with Valentina. And it has been far too long since we've seen her.

Ever recently welcomed three new residents—human women—called here by our Keeper. Almost immediately, all three found monster mates within Ever's wards.

I'm jealous. That's my issue. My mate walks a different path from mine. I'd never pull her from her dreams and ambitions. Alessandro and I had our own dreams, which is why we came to Ever. But I'd like the day to come when Fate aligns our paths together into one, twining us into a tangled but permanent three-way knot. It has to happen eventually. I have to believe that.

Lost in thought, I don't notice I'm at the door to the coffee shop until Higher Grounds swings it open for me.

"Thoughtful girl," I murmur to my store, rubbing the door frame with an elbow to let her know I'm appreciative. The tiny bell above the door dings, announcing my presence.

My employee, Carolya, smiles at me, rounding the counter to take the blooms from my arms.

"Busy morning, Boss!" she chirps, translucent pixie wings fluttering at her back. Like all pixies, her primary job is to work in the pixie dust factory in the Community Garden. That dust powers Ever's protective wards—it's highly important work. I'm lucky to steal her for a few shifts per week.

I glance around the coffee shop. As always, when Carolya's working, it's spic and span. Everything is refilled, clean, and working properly.

"I wish you could teach Alessandro a thing or two about your process," I tease. Except it's not really a joke. We both know Alé might be the charmer of the two of us, but neat and tidy he is *not*.

Carolya snorts. "Good thing you've got me here to sort it out. The espresso machine was sputtering and spewing everywhere when I arrived."

I grin, patting her shoulder, careful not to touch her anywhere that might seem inappropriate. "Indeed, friend. Thank the gods for your assistance."

She beams, cheeks blushing pink, before turning from me. I trail her behind the counter, where she sets the flowers down and begins separating the giant bouquet into three smaller ones. One for the pickup counter, another for the front entryway, and one I'll take upstairs to Alé.

As she works, the steady thrum of Carolya's blood, the way it eddies and swirls through her veins, calls my fangs. She's always relaxed here at work, her heartbeat the same fast thud as all the pixies. Around us, our patrons' conversations reach my ears, overwhelming my senses with scents and whispered sweet nothings. It all serves to drag my mind back to what I was thinking about when I left Fleur.

Movement catches my attention. The ceiling tiles are rippling, cascading outward from a delicate chandelier in the middle of the space.

Carolya chuckles. "The shop likes your new bouquet, Pietro. Well done. The blood-colored roses are a nice touch."

I smile, patting the countertop lovingly.

No, I don't miss Azuro. I love Ever, and I love Higher Grounds.

I miss Valentina. I hope whatever—or whoever—she's doing, she's happy and having fun.

3
ALESSANDRO

"How long will you be in town for?" I grin at Valentina's hologram, hovering above the communication disk on the floor.

She lifts her chin, eyes moving upward as she considers my question. When she returns her gaze to me, her grin is wickedly sensual. "At least a week, perhaps two. What do you think, Alé? It will be good to see each other, even if we aren't hiding away in a tiny haven on the edge of nowhere."

Her words are a match striking the tinder of my lust. That last visit where we holed up in a room and didn't come out? It was everything for Pietro and me.

"Stay forever," I growl, reaching down to adjust my erection.

Her expression softens. "I can't do that. I've just been given this huge project. If I can do this, I'll be able to ask her to make me Chief Haven Designer."

Pride tempers my lustful thoughts, and I smile at her, crossing my arms over my chest to highlight how fit they are. "You've been working toward this for a very long time, my sweet. I'm proud of you. And I have the utmost confidence."

Her cheeks blush slightly pink. "I need you, Alé," she whispers. "I miss you both terribly."

"Good." I reach down and rub my hand down the length of my erect cock. "Come get a taste quickly, my love. We'll be ready the moment you are."

Twin fangs descend from her upper jaw, poking at her plump lower lip.

"Yes," I murmur. "Let me tell you everything we'll do to you. We built a playroom just for your next visit."

"I can't wait to see it." Behind her, there's faint movement, and someone calls her name. She glances over her shoulder, waving at the other monster. When she returns her focus to me, I know she has to go.

"See you soon," I say quietly.

"Soon, mate," she whispers just before clicking off.

As her hologram disappears into the round disk, I consider how long it's been since we took a vacation to see her. Too long. And now she's coming here. She's never been to Ever… I must tell Pietro at once.

Glancing at the ceiling, I beam as I run both hands through slicked-back black hair. "Darling girl, is Pietro back from his chores?"

The kitchen windows open and shut rapidly—a yes.

"Ah, excellent." I swoop down to grab the hologram disk and replace it in its holder on the wall.

Anticipatory nerves jangle through me as I cross the open-floor-plan apartment Pietro and I share. I yank the door open and jog down two flights of stairs to the coffee shop. I must tell him this news at once. She's coming, our mate. I can't wait.

A line of customers trails to the door. Carolya and Pietro are an efficient pair, working hard to brew the various concoctions our patrons adore.

Still, I grab his arm and yank him through a doorway into the back storeroom.

Crimson eyes flash at me, the mirror of mine. Like me, his hair is dark, gelled away from a face with elegant, angular figures. We could be twins. We're not. A quick look at the swirls on our necks would show we're not even related. But we grew up together, even closer than blood brothers.

His crimson eyes narrow as he taps a foot anxiously. "Customers out the door, Alé. Is something wrong?"

I shake my head vigorously. "Valentina is coming, Pietro. She'll be here for a week, possibly two. For work, of course, but still…"

He blinks rapidly, expression going blank.

"She comm'd just now," I say with a grin. "Shall I give you the details while we work?"

He's still blinking. He must be in shock. His heart races, one ear twitching—a nervous habit that carried over from childhood. Reaching inside his collared shirt, he fingers his ziol, the bloodletting cross he'll gift Valentina on the day we formally claim her.

Grinning, I spin him by the shoulders and shove him out of the storeroom. After guiding him to the espresso machine, I take my place at the prep station, grabbing a ticket. "Finish your order," I direct. "I'll share the details."

The hum and buzz of dozens of waiting patrons snap him out of his reverie. He grabs two cups and continues with the drinks.

I grab the nearest container of green troll whip topping and place a dollop on the closest order to me. Then I examine the next few tickets.

Pietro clears his throat.

I grin, fangs poking my lower lip as I speak. "She's coming to speak with Abemet and Catherine about designing and building a new haven outside of Firenze. Apparently, Azuro has grown too large, but they don't necessarily want to recreate Azuro with the new haven. She's been put in charge of designing the new location. It's a huge step for her."

A muscle tightens in Pietro's jaw.

I'm certain he's thinking of the last time we saw her. We spent a sultry weekend tangled up in each other. Every chance we get to come together, it's sensual and perfect. Knowing he's thinking of that makes me hot.

"I invited her to stay with us," I say, "but her work already made reservations at the Annabelle Inn. She's meeting with Catherine there." Our haven's singular BnB is system-renowned for her beauty.

Pietro grunts.

My brother has always been a male of few words. I'm the charmer, sprinkling magic on our romantic trio. Together we create a perfect harmony.

For half an hour, we work in silence. Carolya chirps happily with the customers. Pietro is as quick and efficient as ever.

Eventually, he looks at me, a frown marring his handsome features.

I sigh playfully. "I thought you'd be more excited. Remember that weekend in Vizelle?"

He runs a hand through his hair, slicking back a singular wayward lock. "It's been a long time, Alessandro. Vizelle was eight years ago."

I growl low. "And you remember how perfect she was for us?" I step closer to him, bringing my lips to his ear. "Remember how we filled her together, stretching that sweet pussy until she came?"

Pitch-black lashes flutter against his white cheeks. He blushes, his second eyelid rolling over both eyes in a flash. Ah, his emotions are high. He likes it when I talk about how hot it is when we fuck her.

"How could I forget that?" Scarlet eyes come to mine and narrow. "How are you feeling about this news, brother?"

I beam at him. "I cannot wait to tease you both. I cannot wait to *see* her. And I cannot wait to be naked in our playroom."

Elegant, claw-tipped fingers come to the ziol necklace once

more. Perhaps our paths are finally coming together along the same trajectory. It feels like fate that Valentina is coming to our chosen haven.

Perhaps we will finally cement a relationship that started hundreds of years ago. Perhaps she will finally blood-bind me so I feel them both in the way they already feel one another.

I have been waiting for that my entire life.

Pietro still hasn't responded to my sensual promise.

I kick his boot playfully. "You've got a few hours to muster your excitement, brother. She is coming to dinner tomorrow night."

His mouth drops open, and he fumbles the troll whip container in his hands, dropping it. The glass breaks on the floor, creamy green troll whip covering his lower legs.

I snort in amusement. This is just the beginning of my teasing.

∼

Hours later, dinner warms in the oven as I wait for Pietro to return from his shift downstairs. I spent the afternoon cleaning and preparing for Valentina's arrival. But now? Now it's time to tease my mate.

By the time Valentina gets here, I want Pietro nearly feral. I love the way he commands us when he's at the end of his rope. It starts with me reminding him just how good it feels when she fucks us.

Groaning, I stare down at the automatic blow job toy I recently purchased. He and I share it, and even the idea of *that* makes me hot. I love to take it after he's used it and feel how sloppy it is, filled with his seed.

Blood would be better, but seed is intoxicating.

My fangs descend at that idea. Groaning, I bring the swirling toy down over the tip of my cockhead. The spongy tip of my dick throbs with need as the silicone mimics the hot wetness of a mouth. I watch, fascinated, as the first inch disappears inside the toy. The tube is translucent, so I can stare as the tiny bumps run their way over and around my sensitive skin.

Heat flares through me, balls tightening and filling painfully as I tease just the first part of my length. I'm waiting for Pietro to return home before I tease him with the rest.

On cue, the front door opens, and he stalks through, elegant as always despite a full day's work downstairs. He brings the scent of our coffee with him. I love that smell. Sighing, I breathe in deeply, pulling the memory of Azuro hills covered in coffee trees. We grew up working on a coffee farm in Azuro. The scent of Azuro dark roast always takes me home.

Pietro pauses in the doorway, crimson eyes dropping to the toy. I bring it fully off my cock, gripping it by the base. When I guide it back in, he crosses the room and drops to his knees before me.

"Alé," he whispers, following the path of the toy as it slurps my cock back inside the swirling tube.

"Yes, mate?" I give him a teasing, desperate smile. Our relationship isn't nearly as physical as ours with Valentina. We've never been deeply called to one another in that way, although we dabble on occasion. But vampires are so inherently sexual, we cannot help but tease.

I guide the toy off my length again, and he grips my base, holding me steady while I bring it all the way down. The toy's motor whirs as it struggles to contain all of me. But, gods, the bumps tease every inch of my dick as Pietro's hand tightens around it.

"Remember how she rode me in Vizelle?" I choke out, arching my back at the incessant mechanical pleasure of the toy. I force my eyes open and drop them to Pietro, whose scarlet gaze is locked firmly on my cock.

"How could I ever forget?" he murmurs. "Watching this glorious cock disappear inside her haunts my dreams."

I roll my hips, holding the toy steady as he watches me fuck into it.

"Lick it," I command. "Pretend it's her sweet pussy. Pretend it's the first time you've tasted her in eight years, and you're about to explode."

He grunts and leans forward and down, bringing his mouth to the opening of the toy. On my next thrust in, his tongue drags up the underside of my cock, shocking me with its softness. I grunt and yank the toy all the way to my base, throbbing deep inside it as heat builds fast, too fast.

But Pietro grabs the toy and pulls it off my dick, replacing the suction with his mouth. I gasp, the noise morphing into a moan as he swallows me to the back of his throat and down. His long, soft tongue curls around my cock and rubs in circles that drive me to the edge of sanity.

Reaching down, I thread my fingers through his hair, marveling at the dip of his head as he sucks me off. It's been so long since he did this, maybe even decades. But logical thought escapes me when he pulls off me with a pop and licks at the opening to the toy. I spear back into it, rubbing my cock against his tongue as I fuck the toy with a fast jolt of my hips.

"I'm going to come," I manage as I yank the toy up and down my length.

Pietro's rough fingers come to my sack and squeeze, forcing a guttural cry from deep in my chest. I smash the button to put the toy on its fastest suction mode. Within moments, cum shoots down my shaft, and I empty a full load into the tube, grunting and gasping in pleasure.

Pietro rubs my sack, milking it as I fill the toy, cum streaming down my cock and making his grip sloppy. When he dives down and sucks my sack into his mouth, thoroughly cleaning me, I groan, my grip on his hair tightening.

"You must miss her terribly," I tease, moaning at the feel of his soft, talented tongue sucking my balls clean.

He drops them with a soft pop of his lips. Scarlet eyes come to mine and flash with need. Understanding his look, I step my knees out wide, baring myself for his bloodlust.

Pietro strikes like a viper, sinking his fangs into my inner thigh right by the base of my cock. He deposits venom as he bites, and that bite supercharges my lust, my cock slapping against his face as a second orgasm barrels through me. He sucks and sucks, groaning at my thick blood on his tongue. I cry and pant as pleasure swarms over me, everything driving to the twin prick points of his fangs.

When he's sated enough to release the bite, he pulls back, admiring the slightly bleeding wounds on my darker skin.

"You taste delicious, Alé." His tone is heady with lust and need. When Valentina gets here tomorrow, he'll be in rare form. I can already tell. Having her between us turns Pietro into an animal.

I love it.

And I can't wait.

4

VALENTINA

Interhaven portal travel is always so disconcerting, even though I do it regularly for work. I should be used to walking through the chilly green tunnels that connect our havens into a complicated network. But, goddess, I forgot just how far it was to Ever. Six different connections, six different portals. Someone should really do something about that. The design was originally created that way to beef up security, but there are far better ways.

My designer's mind gets to work on the concept of a central hub, much like the humans' Grand Central Station in New York City. It would be far more convenient for travel than what we have now.

As I step into the final green portal tube, I think about Alessandro and Pietro. We're having dinner tonight, and I can't wait. I toss my long blonde hair over my shoulder as nerves begin to bundle in my stomach. Eesh, I am ready for a drink.

As I step out of the portal into a cavernous building full of windows, I smile. The Ever portal station reminds me of a human train station. I went to one once just to see it.

Being in the same haven as my mates means I can feel Pietro

in our mate bond. I can't wait to see them so I can touch Alé too. I push my excitement at arriving through our bond. Pietro can't wait to see me, but he's...anxious.

That makes two of us.

Not for the first time, I lament not being able to feel Alé that way. One day I will. One day, when the stars align to put us together more consistently, I'll sink my fangs into him, spilling my venom into his body to create a blood bond just as powerful as the one Pietro and I share.

Gripping my single bag tightly, I cross to the building's exit. Monsters of all species come and go in a rush; this is a busy haven. One of the most successful, according to Hearth HQ reporting. I'd like to learn more about why that is so I can recreate the magic. I have meetings with the former Keeper and Catherine to ask questions, but I can't wait to explore for a week or two to see why Ever is so beloved among the havens in our system.

When I exit, I notice the air here is a touch brisker than my home haven of Azuro, but decidedly warmer than Hearth HQ's weather. It's smack dab between pleasant and lovely. I pull a small notebook from the pocket of my fitted slacks and jot something down.

"Sixty-eight degrees," a smooth voice offers. "Perfetto, don't you think?"

Everything inside me seems to tighten and unfurl at the same time, lazy pleasure filling my core. *That voice.* I could pick him blindfolded out of a room of a thousand vampire males. Damn, we've done just that in orgies in vamp clubs in quite a few havens.

Grinning, I look up. Alé sits in front of me on a moped. Black hair is smoothed back from a hawkish, elegant face. Crimson eyes cast a quick, appreciative glance down my figure before he draws them back up with a genuine expression. He wears a seemingly permanent smile. Is that what his emotions are like on the inside? I imagine him to be full of joy twenty-four hours a day. I want to know. I want the bond that will tell me how he's feeling.

"It's lovely, Alé," I agree, walking toward him as I shove my notebook back into my pocket. Without really meaning to, I drag my wavy hair away from my neck, baring it for him to see. Actually, I did mean to do that. He loves staring at my neck. Nuzzling my neck. Biting my neck.

And I adore it when he does all of those things.

His smile grows impish.

When I stop in front of him, he slips gracefully off the moped and reaches for my bag, pulling me with his free arm into a tight hug. At the barest hint of his mouth near my skin, I light up, body tightening. I arch and sink into him, head falling to one side.

An invitation. Gods, I never could resist him. Of the two of them, Alé teases the most. I'm a sucker for my men—I give in immediately. And Pietro? Pietro gets bossy and demanding.

Alé's hand flattens against my back as he angles his face to the side, burying his nose beneath my hair. "Just like I remember, Valentina," he murmurs. "Let's skip dinner and get right to dessert. What do you say?"

I can't find anything *to* say. I've taken lovers since I last saw him—blood and sex are too connected for vampires. But no short-lived dalliance could ever be what I have with him and Pietro. That's why I couldn't take that male from the bar home. There's something so familiar, so easy and deep with males I've known my entire life. I need more of *that*.

I don't answer his question, though. Instead, I pose one of my own. "Where's Pietro?"

Alessandro straightens, scarlet eyes flashing with what I imagine is amusement. "Working. I'll drop you at the Annabelle Inn, but he'll be around for dinner. Perhaps you should send him a sexy little message through your bond, eh?"

When he winks, I blush, but my focus goes to the bond with

Pietro. Now, lazy swirls of heat fill it, tightening my body. He knows Alé has me.

Alé turns and secures my bag to the back of his moped. Reaching out, he takes my hand and pulls me carefully onto the seat in front of him. The moped is designed for two riders, but I still find myself cocooned within large, muscular arms that feel at once familiar and new.

Hologram communication never does him justice. In person, everything about him is…more. Bigger, sexier, more delicious. Confident and charming but genuine and rock-steady. Alé is perfection.

He pats my thigh. "Do you have a headscarf, amore?"

"Frontmost pocket of my bag," I say over my shoulder. The sound of him rustling through my bag drifts forward.

Big hands come to my scalp and card my hair back into a low ponytail. I hold it in place as he drapes the headscarf over my hair. When I drop my head forward to give him access, I tense at the vulnerable position. Having Alé's warm body behind me like this, focused on me? I can't wait for dinner.

He leans forward, his muscular chest pressed to my back as he ties the headscarf at the base of my neck. Warm lips come to a spot at the top of my shoulder and press, sending a flash of heat through me. Alé brings his mouth to my ear. "Hold on tight, amore."

With a quick rev, we jerk into motion, taking off up a wide street.

Brisk wind buffets my face, but he keeps the speed pleasant enough for me to take in our surroundings. I studied a map of this haven, Ever, before I arrived. The portal station sits within Shifter Hollow, a section of town dedicated to shifters, centaurs and pegasi. Everything here is built with those monsters in mind, something to consider as I begin planning another haven. I'll need to spend some time in this part of the haven, comparing it to the main downtown area that has a more traditional layout.

Twenty minutes later, dense redwood forest gives way to a smattering of buildings.

Alessandro pats my thigh carefully. When I look, he points to a darling three-story coffee shop to our right.

"Higher Grounds, our shop." He points ahead. "The Annabelle is just there across from the Community Garden where the pixies live. Our pixie dust is made there." He gestures to the side. "Most of the other establishments are that way, heading out of town."

I resist the urge to hop off the moped and go see Pietro now. Gods know I'd like to. The last time we parted nearly killed all three of us. So many tears. But now I'm here. And it has been far too long. Eight years and seventeen days since I've seen them. Now that I'm safely within the cocoon of Alé's arms, it's terrible to consider leaving.

Alessandro presses us forward, crossing a big street. I glance around in wonder. It's lined with buildings, monsters of all species walking up and down the sidewalks. I'm so excited to learn more about this haven. Its appearance is far different from my home haven or Hearth HQ. Homey in a very retro, American way.

Moments later, we pull up in front of a beautiful two-story pink building with white gingerbread trim and white shutters. A sign naming her The Annabelle Inn sits on the corner. A street full of homes sits just past the Annabelle, a brightly colored garden visible across the street.

The front doors swing open in greeting, white shutters waggling a happy hello.

I smile and wave to the inn as Alessandro helps me off the moped.

He leans down and presses a tender kiss to my cheek. "Welcome to Ever, Valentina."

5
PIETRO

I pour a cup of coffee, fingers trembling slightly. She's here, somewhere in the same haven as us. The coffee spills over the edge, dribbling hot down my fingers as I hiss and gnash my fangs at my clumsiness. After setting the pot back on the heater, I wipe my hands on my pants as Alé comes out of the storeroom.

He dropped her off hours ago so she could get settled before her meetings. I haven't even seen her yet.

She's been busy and focused; I've felt that.

My brother bumps me with his hip. "Tell me what she's feeling right now."

It's a game we like to play, since he can't yet feel her through a bond between them.

"She's excited," I whisper. "Ready to see us."

Alé lets out a soft, needy groan, eyes rolling back in his head as he grins. When he's done with that, he brings his focus to mine. "Seeing her is like coming home. I cannot wait to watch you both when she sees you for the first time."

As if on cue, the front door bell dings cheerfully.

In a moment, all the air is sucked from the room, and time

slows. A thread somewhere deep in my chest yanks and tugs, forcing my eyes toward the front of the shop. A curvaceous figure stands in the doorway, framed by fading sunlight. She wears thigh-hugging black slacks, elegant strappy heels, and a bustier that shoves her gorgeous breasts up. A transparent lacy sweater gives her a sort of sexy librarian vibe. Wavy blond hair is pinned into a messy bun on top of her head.

Fuck.

I'm here for it.

I'm here for any of it. All of it. I need to bite Alé while I fuck her and then switch positions and do it all again. I've been running extra hot since he and I played last night.

"Valentina," I whisper.

Time stops completely, sound muffling as her ruby eyes meet mine. She moves gracefully across the space. Do I imagine her hips swaying so sensually? Was she always this intoxicating? My mind blinks, then roars to life again when she stops on the other side of the counter.

She has to look up to meet my gaze. Heady possession and need scramble my thoughts when she reaches across the counter to squeeze my forearm, eyes wrinkling at the corners. Alé is a ghost by my side, grinning, I'm sure. He's all smiles when she's around.

She squeezes my arm. "Pietro, it's been too long!"

Understatement of the century. Our last coming-together barely sated the soul-deep thirst I have for her. Alé and I took her for days, burying our fangs in every inch of her glorious body. And then, because we were all focused on our individual dreams, we moved on.

Well, they moved on. I think.

I struggled with it. Just like now. It's hard not to pull her over the counter into my embrace, sinking my fangs into the beautiful vein that travels down the side of her throat. To drop my ziol necklace over her head, tuck it between her breasts, and then put a claiming mark on her skin.

She must sense my scattered thoughts in our bond. Her smile turns into a smirk, fingers curled around my forearm.

"Valentina," I murmur. "You made it!" I force cheerfulness into my voice as I attempt to get my thoughts together.

She brightens. "Yes! I'm settled at the Annabelle, and now I'm headed to the Historical Society to speak with the former Keeper about what sets Ever apart from other havens. The growth rate here is truly unparalleled."

I smirk at that. Our previous Keeper—Ever's de facto mayor of sorts—is best in class. He's made this place safe and welcoming for all. That's why monsters of all species flock to Ever. There's even a harpy who lives in Shifter Hollow, and that is truly amazing. The solitary monsters traditionally shun the haven system, preferring to live in the wild and take their chances.

Valentina nips at her lower lip, drawing my focus there. "Alessandro invited me to dinner. Is that alright? I'd love to catch up…" her voice trails off, breathy and expectant.

Our bond lights up with lust as I grip the countertop, focus narrowing on her neck where that gorgeous vein throbs.

"We can't wait," Alé says quietly, saving me from myself.

I can barely summon the strength to look up from the tiny twin fangs that peek out from under her plump upper lip. I've had those fangs buried in every inch of my body. Something pangs and twinges deep in my chest.

Dismay. Concern.

I run both hands through my hair. I'm not being a very good mate.

"Of course," I say smoothly, forcing my voice not to waver. My fingers twitch with the need to touch her. "We'll cook something delicious. Our loft is upstairs on the top floor. Come back whenever you're done with your meetings."

"Okay." She lifts a hand to rub at her chest.

I need to touch her. I have to. Slipping over the counter, I ignore the stares from our patrons as I slide my arms around her waist and pull her body flush with mine. She sinks easily into my embrace, lashes fluttering as she lifts her gaze upward.

Dipping down low, I press my lips to hers, keeping my eyes open so I can stare at her. She's even more beautiful than last time we met, her supple figure familiar and intoxicating. My protective eyelid flashes over my eyes, and she moans quietly into the soft kiss.

After a long, tender moment, she steps back, chest heaving as she stares at me.

Does she feel the increasing need to formalize our mating like I do? Does she know and shove that bond aside to pursue her work? Is she so busy, so fulfilled in her life at Hearth HQ that she isn't consumed by the idea of us the way I am, the way Alé is?

I don't have the answers to any of those questions. But as she says goodbye and turns to go, I wonder if, perhaps, we'll get them tonight.

6

VALENTINA

Fuck. I don't even want to do meetings now at all. I came here for research, but having my mates right here has me supremely distracted. Still, I can't afford not to kick ass on this project. Evenia will give me the promotion if I'm successful in designing the new haven. But if I fail? Public humiliation is the least of what she'll do to me.

I walk the length of Main Street, which runs in front of Pietro and Alessandro's coffee shop, Higher Grounds. This haven is adorable. Red and white awnings top every building's entrance. Flowers dangle from lamp posts lining the street all the way to the end where the Historical Society sits.

I'm meeting my contact there. As I walk past a shop called Fleur, bursting at the seams with flowers, I consider how it felt to see Pietro and Alessandro for the first time in so long. A nearly painful tug in my chest urges me to return to my men. Rubbing at my chest, I consider how the building desire will only serve to make tonight more delicious.

It feels impossible to wait a few hours to touch them. As I walk toward my destination, everything seems heightened. My sensitive ears pick up all the conversations around me, my nose taking in smells from every store on the street. I'd like to pull out my shadow wings and fly back to the coffee shop, tackle Alé and wait for Pietro to tell us what he wants us to do.

Shuddering, I force myself to rein it in as I pass the movie theater and find a small, singular stone building with a beautiful garden out front.

My contact, Abemet, stands out front with both hands slung in his pockets. He's a vampire too—Evenia's son, actually. I've met him a few times. It's clear they don't get along, but perhaps it's because they're similar in quite a few ways.

"Keeper, hello," I croon as I walk up the path with a smile.

He returns the expression and grabs the door, opening it for me. "It's just Abemet now, Valentina. I'm no longer Ever's Keeper…it's been a while."

A while indeed. The last time I saw him, he had just returned from the human world to meet his mother about something. He seemed stressed then. Now he seems…neutral. Well-masked. Of course, the Keeper training does that to those with the right magic. They're never quite the same afterward. I can expect him to be uncomfortably blunt. But then, I've met plenty of Keepers at headquarters, so this is nothing I can't handle.

He follows me through into the library section of the Historical Society. It's quiet here, a few beings seated at tables with giant dusty tomes in front of them. I smile at a centaur resting on a curved bench that supports the horse part of his body. He winks at me as I walk past.

Gods, I dated a centaur briefly at HQ, but he was far too focused on settling down. And, of course, I would never have wanted that with him.

Abemet strides ahead of me, pointing toward a door at the far back of the building. I follow him through it into an honest-to-gods classroom.

He shoots me a half smile. "Figured it would be nice to have the chalkboard to draw out anything that needs it. But, depending on how things go, we can move this meeting to Herschel's and get you some lunch."

Grinning, I stare at the rows of desks, setting my bag down. Rubbing my hands together, I allow excitement to fill me, my eyes flashing at the other vampire. "Excellent. Let us get started."

Yet, hours later, we're still in the classroom. Abemet stands at the chalkboard with a piece of chalk in his hands, sketching out a rough map of the haven as he speaks about the number of square acres per monster the shifter pack alpha recommended. It's nearly double the standard guideline.

"You think it's worked better, though? That the Hearth HQ guideline is too small?"

He nods. "Richard, our pack alpha, primarily grew up in Arcadia and Santa Alaya, so he was accustomed to a huge space. But the Shifter Hollow monsters on the far side of town all rate the space highly when we do surveys."

I mull that over. "I wonder what else could be improved if we took a look at the guidelines again."

Abemet stands quietly, giving me a moment to process my thoughts.

I glance up at him. "On an unrelated note, I've been considering something for the last few months. Can I float an idea past you?"

Another clipped nod gives me the go-ahead.

As I lay my idea out, his expression becomes resigned. Once I'm done with it, he sighs. "I would love for that to be the case, but Evenia has always been incredibly resistant to it. But," he tosses a half smile in my direction, "if anybody can convince her otherwise, it would be you."

Pride fills me. It's well known that I'm Evenia's favorite direct report. I don't really know how I got to be in that position, other than playing the headquarters politics game well. But, regardless, if it means I can get things done for my fellow monsters, for my mates, it's all worth it.

Another hour later, I leave with reams of notes from our meeting. Returning to the Annabelle Inn, I sequester myself in my rose-themed room and sketch out ideas until the sun begins to set. My bond with Pietro is quiet. Like always, he is giving me space to work.

Thoughtful, beautiful mate.

By the time the comm watch at my wrist pings, letting me know it's time for dinner, nerves have begun to clang in my belly, and I lose focus on my sketches. More than that, the tug in my chest has become impossible to ignore.

The Inn must sense my scattered thoughts, because she tosses the closet doors open and begins flinging outfits out at me.

Laughing, I stalk to the options and grin. They're all so sexy. See-through cardigans and tight skirts. High heels and beautiful V-neck tops.

Merciless need unfurls in our bond, filling it with anticipation and excitement. It's time.

I pick from Annabelle's choices, dressing in a flowy top that cuts to my navel, cleavage teasing from beneath the fabric. A translucent sweater goes over top of that, and then a knee-length fitted skirt and heels to top it off. Glancing in the mirror, I pile my hair into a messy bun on top of my head. When that's done, I pat the wall.

"Thank you, darling Annabelle. Your taste in date night attire is most excellent."

The wallpaper ripples happily, forcing my smile wider. The Annabelle Inn is system-renowned for her beauty and personality. I haven't had a chance to see it up close, but it's clear there is *so much love* in this building.

Hearth HQ isn't like that. A few of the buildings have personality, but the headquarters building itself is stark and reserved, almost grumpy. It's true that every building is different, but to me, headquarters feels like its mistress—cold, unwelcoming and unfriendly.

Once I'm ready, I depart the Annabelle, who waves her white shutters in goodbye. The Community Garden is located across the street, and I consider going there to take a peek. The pixies' A-frame neighborhood is built there, a unique design that, as far as I know, is only done in this particular haven. Plus, the pixie dust factory is located in the garden's only tree. I'd like to know more about that.

But then Pietro tugs sensually at our bond, and I decide I'll tackle the garden tomorrow. I need my males right now.

Humming happily, I walk the few blocks up Sycamore, cross Main and enter Higher Grounds. Even at dinner time, the shop is full of patrons.

Pride fills me—Alé and Pietro have done so well. This is what they always wanted, to bring coffee to the world. To have a gathering place for the monster community. I can almost imagine them working the shop together. Alé would be all charming smiles and flirtations. Pietro would be the quiet, intense presence by his side.

With a smile, I head for the stairs, jogging upward until I reach the third floor. A single arched wooden door reminds me of home—whitewashed wood is cracked and faded around the edges. The hallway is painted a terra cotta shade, much like the roof tiles from the villa I grew up in. Even up here, everything smells of Azuro coffee beans.

It feels like home.

The door swings open, revealing Alé wearing a happy smile. He pats the door. "Imported from the family villa. Beautiful, isn't it?"

I stroke the door, admiring the ancient-looking wood. The building creaks and groans, the surface vibrating under my touch.

"She's ticklish," he jokes, grabbing my hand. "Come in, amore."

Amore.

Such an innocuous word used between mothers and sons, fathers and daughters, friends, lovers. It can be used in nearly any context.

But we were never *just* friends. When he says that word to me, I feel it in every corner of my being. I tamp down the urge to tackle him and bite over his heart, infusing my venom into the organ that pumps blood throughout his body. I want it to be full of me, threaded so deeply, we can never be parted.

My bond with Pietro tenses and tightens as he registers my emotion and intention. It's what he wants most…for us to be together all the time.

I want that too, but I don't see a way to have it unless someone gives up their dreams. That's been a hard series of acts to juggle over the centuries. But I can't think about that tonight. Tonight is about reconnection.

Varied scents fill the air just inside the door—salt, basil, a few others that remind me of home. I spin in place, admiring the huge open living area. The back and right-hand walls are full of windows, letting in beautiful fading sunlight. Couches and rugs in a mishmash of colors litter the space, giving it a homey feel. The back wall features a kitchen with a large whitewashed island.

Pietro stands there, both hands on the countertop, chest heaving slightly as he stares at me. A pot bubbles behind him. Gods, he's stunning. His desire to command me slaps our bond as he yanks on it, pulling me across the room with near physical touch.

I grab Alé's hand, cross the space, and round the island, halting in front of Pietro. He turns slowly, dark eyes dropping appreciatively down my body. Alessandro presses his chest to my back, shoving me closer to our mate. Warm lips come to my ear. "It's been a long time, Valentina. We have missed you terribly."

That thing in my chest connecting me to Pietro sparks and sputters, demanding to be filled, touched, used, claimed.

He grits his jaw tightly but reaches up and strokes my hair away from my forehead. What I can't read in his expression, I feel in the bond we share.

Adoration. Desire. Pride.

Desperate, unrelenting need.

7
ALESSANDRO

Watching my two favorite people together brings me peace. I love the life Pietro and I have built, but it's incomplete without her between us. That's never been clearer than right now with Pietro in front of her, stroking her hair as he eats her alive with his gaze.

"I want to kiss you," he growls, "but if I start now, I don't think I'll make it through dinner." He steps closer, bringing his mouth just over hers, which forces her head back against my shoulder. "I need to watch you fuck him, bite him, toy with him. And then I want you on your knees before me, worshipping."

Her chest heaves as I slip transparent fabric off her delicate shoulder. When I reach down and place a tender trail of kisses on her soft, warm skin, she shudders between us.

"Alé, stop," Pietro commands, his voice hard as steel. "Or I will lose my mind."

"Don't lose it yet," I tease, "your pasta sauce is boiling over."

Pietro growls, hesitating as he watches me drag my tongue up Valentina's neck. A desperate mewl erupts from his throat, but the pasta sauce boils and hisses as it hits the hot stove. He spins away from us as I chuckle into our mate's neck.

She pulls me with her toward him, yanking Pietro's perfectly tailored shirt out of the back of his pants. When she slides both hands underneath it to touch him, he groans and shoves the pasta sauce off the burner.

"I have to touch you both," she whispers. "Please let me."

Pietro snarls and turns, focused on her as he unbuttons his vest and tosses it away. Her hands rove his upper body, greedily stroking him.

Not for the first time, I wish I could feel that bond between them. Every time we get together, we talk about her biting me. And every time, it's me who makes the final determination that I'm not ready. It's hard enough when we part, and I see how it destroys Pietro for months. I might be Mister Confidence, but I don't think I have the inner strength to watch her walk away, to feel that bond go dark when she disappears through the portal and returns to her life.

But then Pietro shrugs his shirt off, revealing a muscular upper body covered in tattoos. Valentina moans softly, fingers dancing over the dark ink on his pale skin. She trails the tattoo of his core family line down to his upper pec.

"Bite him," I encourage, slipping a hand between them to rub my fingertips over his heart.

Pietro growls, fangs descending as his second lid rolls over his eye. The chunky ziol necklace hanging between his chest muscles glints and gleams in the light. I've never seen a ziol as beautiful as the one we paid for together when we had enough money. Some days I wear it, but I prefer to see it on him.

"May I?" Valentina's sweet request has his jaw clenching, muscles popping.

If she bites him now, he'll come. And fuck dinner, because we'll be on the floor first and then the playroom next.

"No," he states, his voice full of command. He tips her chin up. "Did you eat? Are you hungry?"

Hungry for blood, I want to snap. But in the bedroom, he commands us.

And we fucking love it.

It's always been that way. I'll never forget how shy he was as a younger male, but as he became a man, a dominance arose in him when we three were alone. It started as a dare one night. Valentina teased him to tell us what to do. But then it felt so right, so good, so hot, we expanded on that over the years.

In public, Pietro seems to be the quieter, more subservient personality. But it's all an act. Because our Pietro in the bedroom is a monstrously commanding force.

On cue, Valentina's stomach rumbles, and he gives her a sideways look. "Mate…tell me the truth. Did you eat?"

She shakes her head no, and that's all he needs to move away from us and return to the pot that now simmers on the stove.

"Sit." He waves us toward the table. "We must feed you first, mate. Sex second."

"Awww," I tease, nipping at her neck playfully. "Fine."

Valentina turns to me with wickedness in her smile. "If our mate won't kiss me, Alé, perhaps you will?"

I am not the man Pietro is, because I cannot find it in me to deny our woman what she so sweetly asks for. Bending down, I run my hands over the firm globes of her ass, bringing my forehead to hers. Sliding down her body, I grip the backs of her thighs and pull her up onto our kitchen island.

Pietro growls as he dishes pasta sauce into a saucepan of homemade noodles.

Ignoring his ire, I push my mate's skirt up her beautiful pale thighs until I can spread them wide enough to wrap her legs around my waist. She smiles sensually up at me, slinging an arm around my neck.

Everything about her is so familiar, so perfect, I can't resist bringing my mouth to her throat. I breathe her in, soaking in a scent that's called to me for hundreds of years. She's all sun-drenched fields mixed with snow-capped mountains and crisp, tart cherries. Growling, I drag my open mouth over her throat, tongue darting out to taste her skin.

So good.

So good.

So *fucking* good.

I can't resist closing my fangs over her throat just under her neck. Her head falls back into my palm as she gasps, opening herself to me, inviting me in.

I bite over and over, softly puncturing her skin, bringing the tiniest of blood droplets to the surface. Pietro groans from across the kitchen.

Licking up the wounds I just made, desperate sounds tumble from my throat at tasting her. My cock throbs painfully inside my pants. Unable to resist, I reach down and stroke it as I bite and lick her neck.

This was supposed to be just a kiss, something to tantalize and tease our mate. But I'm quickly losing control. Mentally slapping myself, I take a step back and away, chest heaving and hand still on my dick.

Valentina's ruby eyes drop to my hand, then she glances at Pietro. "I could skip dinner, mate, if your need is too strong."

He crosses the kitchen in a flash, gripping her cheeks to squeeze her plump lips together. His mouth brushes over hers as he growls, "My job is to take care of you, even when the two of you seem determined to distract me. Eat quickly, and then I will take care of your other needs."

I swat his hand away and kiss her plump lips softly. Pietro returns to the dinner, plating it.

Bringing my lips to her ear, I nip at it. "He sucked me off last night, mate, and it felt so fucking good."

Valentina's groan stiffens my cock as seed fills my balls. I pull back, admiring the needy look on her face.

"I love it when you touch," she admits.

Glancing at Pietro, I cast him a sexy smile. "Hear that, mate? She likes to see us touch."

He smirks as he carries all three plates to our rectangular wood dining table by the side windows.

I pull her off the countertop into my arms, letting her body drag down my erection. We let out matching groans. For a moment, the world stills, and even Pietro disappears as I stare at my mate, so fucking thankful to be with her once more. I move a hand to her elegant wavy bangs, tucking them behind her ear.

"I have missed you greatly," I whisper. "I never want you to leave."

Dark lashes flutter against her cheeks as her mouth drops open. "I know," she whispers. "It gets harder and harder to leave you every time. I…don't want to."

Hope sparks in my chest. Maybe this is the time, finally, when we don't have to choose our dreams over our love.

Pietro sits at the table, an empty chair next to him. As he lays one arm over the back, I know he's calling us to dinner.

Smiling at him in understanding, I tug our mate around the island. I guide her to the chair next to him, and his hand moves immediately to her inner thigh, caressing and squeezing.

Valentina laughs. "Mate, I will never be able to focus on eating if you do that."

Pietro lifts a glass of wine to his lips and takes a sip. After he swallows, he gives her a sensual look that tightens my balls. "I haven't even begun to distract you, Valentina. Eat."

My nostrils flare as his fingers travel farther up her inner thigh until they reach the juncture where it meets her pussy. He strokes as her back arches and she bares her neck to him.

He can't resist. No sane male could. Striking fast, he sinks his teeth into her throat, eyelid rolling over his crimson irises. Pietro roars into the bite as Valentina comes, writhing on the chair as she screams his name. She grips the chair's sides with both hands, muscles trembling as shockwaves bash her, Pietro's fingers moving steadily between her thighs.

Gods, that mate bite is something else. I can't wait to have that. As I watch them come down from tonight's first orgasm, I consider if it's time for me to say I'm ready to be bitten.

"Eat, for the love of gods," Pietro whispers when he releases his bite.

Valentina's chest heaves, her sweater falling off both shoulders as blood dribbles down her skin.

I can't help it. Lurching forward, I lick the blood off her neck. She tastes of Pietro's venom. The smallest bit of it has me dripping precum down my thigh.

"Fuck dinner," I growl, bringing my hand between her legs to slip a finger in next to Pietro's.

"Yes!" she cries out, looking down to where we finger her together. But then her eyes roll into her head, and she begins to writhe against us.

"I have an idea, mate," I offer, looking at Pietro. "You get some sustenance into our woman, and I'll eat something else." I glance meaningfully to where we're fucking her, and Pietro's smile grows wide.

"Do it, brother," he commands.

I don't need any further encouragement than that.

Dropping out of my chair and tucking beneath the table, I pull Valentina's chair closer and shove her thighs wide. Gripping her ass, I pull her to the edge of the chair as Pietro removes his fingers from her pussy.

She wears no underwear, and her shaved pussy glistens with arousal. Her thighs tremble when I grip her ass and lean in to scent her. Above me, Pietro murmurs to her, feeding her, talking to her. I stare for a while. I love staring at her. Knowing she's ours, that the fates made her for us.

My mouth and tongue were made to please her. Smiling, I dip forward and lick softly up her pussy, swirling my tongue around her clit. She jolts and jumps, banging her knee against the underside of the table with a groan. Pietro talks softly to her, encouraging her to eat as I grin and lap at her again.

It's not long before my ministrations grow rough and ragged. I love eating her out, tasting her as her arousal grows, knowing she'll explode with nothing more than my tongue on her clit. When I close my mouth around her sensitive skin and suck, she shoves backward and stares at me from above.

Her thighs tremble as I run my tongue roughly from side to side, then suck at her clit again. She mewls and pants as Pietro brings his lips to her ear and speaks. He tells her how beautiful she is, how much we love her, how much we've missed her, and then she's coming, flooding my mouth with her ecstasy. She pants and clings to Pietro as I eat her through one orgasm. I don't stop when she comes down, heading for the next when Pietro dips down and gives me a look.

"She can't focus on the food. Let's pause for a minute, mate."

Chuckling, I rise from beneath the table, wiping my mouth with the back of my hand.

Valentina stares at me with hooded eyes narrowed with lust. She is on the verge of tossing the table over and tackling me.

But Pietro is right. As hard as it is for me to behave, we need to take care of her.

"Eat, darling," I encourage, eyes flicking to the pasta in front of her. "When you've done that, you can eat me."

Her nostrils flare, a rough growl ripping from her throat.

"Alé…" Pietro cautions. "Enough."

I throw my hands in the air. "Fine, I'll behave."

For a few minutes, at least. Forcing myself to focus on the pasta Pietro made from scratch, I shove noodles in my mouth as he asks her about work.

That topic excites her, and for the next quarter hour she tells us about her current project building a second haven near Azuro. She has distinct thoughts based on her conversation with Abemet earlier. Pietro offers to take her around town tomorrow and give her his perspective. Irritation sparks in my gut at that. I'm working tomorrow, and I just know they'll take time to fuck in the woods somewhere.

I want that. Perhaps I can get Carolya to come in and cover for me so I can join them. It was always like this with us—the three of us drawn together like magnets, pulled constantly into orbit together. I have been in love with Valentina since we came of age and her bond with Pietro appeared. It matters not to me that the traditional vampiric bond didn't pick me. *They* have always picked me.

Valentina sits gracefully in a chair, her legs in Pietro's lap. He strokes one as she drags her nails lazily up my thigh. She hasn't finished dinner, and she's distracted.

Spearing a bite of chicken and pasta, I hold it to her lips. "Open, woman."

Her cheeks flush, ruby eyes sparkling as she opens wide, pink tongue poking out. She takes the bite and chews, wiping at the corners of her mouth. Pietro licks his lips as he watches her eat the food he made for us.

She obeys dutifully, licking the pasta before taking it into her mouth. She teases us as sensually as we tease her. By the time she's full, I have joined Pietro in the lost fight to lust. When Pietro brings her an espresso, it's all I can do not to sweep the entire table's worth of dishes onto the floor and lay her on it as our dessert. He is determined to edge us to the brink of insanity.

She sips at the hot drink, giggling at how different it tastes. Pietro explains some thing or another about the water here in Ever, but I tune it out. The tension between us is obvious, her smell burgeoning and blossoming the more she sips. Does she realize she's squirming in her seat, or that her heart rate continues to rise despite several orgasms?

When I can take it no longer, I shove my chair back. "Let's go to bed," I growl, holding a hand out for her.

Pietro cuts me a sharp look, but the hunger in his eyes is obvious.

Valentina turns to me with a chuckle. "Are you feeling quite needy, Alé? Didn't get enough dinner?" Her voice goes throaty and deep, her fangs descending to poke her lower lip.

I give her a wicked grin. "I need to drink you down, to spill deep inside you, to watch our mate do the same." I wrap my long fingers around her throat.

Dark eyes flash as I pull her from the chair and position her in my lap, her back against my chest. I grind my hard-on against her ass. "Feel that, Valentina?" I squeeze her throat a bit tighter. "And look at Pietro. See how much he wants you?"

In front of us, Pietro shifts backward in his seat, stepping his feet slightly outward. The move accentuates the hard shaft pressed to one thigh, barely hidden by his pants. He grins lazily, his initial focus on dinner finally assuaged. One hand grips his cock, rubbing down it as he stares heatedly at our mate.

Valentina's chest rises and falls fast underneath my forearm. Sliding my free hand up her taut stomach, I caress the underneath of one breast. She groans and drags my hand to her nipple. I pinch and roll it between my fingers as her head falls against my shoulder.

"Ask me to bite you," I purr into her ear, rubbing my dick up the crack of her ass.

She quivers beneath my touch. "Too many clothes," she mutters. "You're both wearing too many clothes."

Pietro stands, reaching for her hand. "Come." His voice is soft, thoughtful, but a command nonetheless.

She takes his hand and mine and follows. I trail them around the island and down the long hall that leads to our rooms. Pietro and I keep separate rooms for sleeping, but a giant open area between them is designed purely for play. We've brought occasional lovers here, but we designed this room with *her* in mind. A sex swing hangs from the corner, and the center of the room has a giant flat play bed.

Pietro drops her hand and stops just shy of us, smirking at me. "Undress her," he commands.

With a needy groan, I round her and pull the translucent sweater all the way off her delicate shoulders. She sighs and leans forward, giving me easy access to the laced back of the bustier.

"I fucking love laces." I unknot the very top and begin to loosen it.

Pietro is a statue, eyes locked onto her as I loosen the garment. When it slips down her body, she's nude beneath it. He and I let out matching groans.

"Look at her," I muse. "Still so beautiful. Still ours."

"Ours," he confirms, crooking two fingers at her. Crimson eyes come to mine. "Take your clothes off, brother. I want you ready for her."

I'll take a command from him any day. Pietro reaches for Valentina's hand and pulls her toward the large velvet-covered bed in the middle of the room.

I rip my shirt off as I trail after them. Her eyes find me as I drop my pants to the ground. Pietro stands with our female in his arms, both of my mates staring at my naked figure. His hands roam every inch of her neck, her back.

"Perfetto," I murmur as I watch them. "You two are perfection."

8
PIETRO

After all this time, she's exactly as I remember. Smooth, supple skin. Delicate, powerful form. That perfectly round, firm ass. In one swift move, I pick Valentina up and crawl onto the giant round cushion, depositing her on her back next to Alessandro as he undresses.

"Bite her," I command, stroking my fingers down her chest.

He opens wide, his second eyelid rolling white over his eyes. Then he strikes like a viper, latching on to her breast and sucking. The heady scent of my mate's blood fills the air, her mouth opening in a silent scream as her back arches. Her hands come to his hair, threading through it as her hips rock.

For a long moment, I allow myself to simply watch them. Pink dusts her cheeks. Scarlet lips are open on a silent howl. Alessandro sucks at her breast, her other nipple pebbled and tight. My mouth waters at the scene before me. There was tension when she first arrived. But this? Now?

This is as it should be. Dipping forward, I kiss her nipple, the tip of my tongue darting out to press against it.

Valentina wails, reaching for me as I hollow my cheeks, sucking her tip into my mouth. Her taste is everything—warm candlelight and decadent tart berries. I move from her breast to the swell underneath, kissing and biting playfully while Alessandro pulls gulp after gulp of blood from her.

The heavy scent of her arousal fills the air, her chest rising and falling as I make my way down her body. When I get to the juncture of her thighs, she begins to tremble. She's still soaked from our earlier play and Alé's tongue.

Persistent tugging in my chest draws my focus back to her face. Ruby eyes watch me intensely, her fangs poking her lower lip. Alessandro releases his bite and groans, licking a flat path over her nipple. The attention makes her writhe, eyes flicking to him, lips curling into a sated smile.

"Watch him enjoy you," Alé commands. "We have wanted this for so long, amore."

My knees hit the floor, and I slide my hands under her legs to her ass, spreading her for me. She's completely smooth, pussy glistening with arousal. I bury my face between her thighs and breathe deeply, soaking in her essence, that scent made to drive me wild.

"Eat, brother," Alé directs. Shifting onto his knees, he grabs his bobbing, leaking cock and pats her gently on the lips. "You too, beautiful girl."

I circle my tongue over her clit just as she opens wide for his rigid length. But the moment my tongue touches her sensitive nub, she moans and falls back against the cushion, eyes rolling into her head.

"Tsk, tsk," Alé chides her with a laugh. "I need your mouth, Valentina."

With a snarl, she surges forward and takes him to the hilt, burying his cock deep in her throat. She clamps down on the base, white eyelids rolling over her irises.

Pleasure swirls heavy and hard in my sack, forcing precum to shoot from my shaft. I can't tear my eyes from them, from the way her venom has Alessandro ready to burst. From the way her body is tense and tight, her clit swollen and needy.

I need her pleasure. Surging forward, I lick a path up her pussy, then suckle gently on her clit in rhythmic waves. Her thighs clamp shut around my head, her muscles trembling as I lick and suck in the teasing pattern she has always loved.

When I slip two fingers inside her pussy and begin to stroke, she explodes, hips thrusting against me as sweet honey floods from her to coat my mouth and chin.

Groaning, I grind my hips against the cushion for some friction, any friction enough to bring me the same ecstasy.

Alé shouts, throwing his head back, both fists wrapped through Valentina's blonde hair. He bellows her name as he fills her throat with so much seed, it dribbles from both sides and down her chin.

I continue my slow torture of her sweet channel. She'll come a half dozen times before I go wild. It was always like that with us. A slow and steady build to insanity, and then the frenzy of blood and brutality she prefers to end with.

Alé laughs triumphantly, grinning at me as he comes down, pulling his dripping cock from between her plump, perfect lips.

This. This is as it should be.

This is home.

9

VALENTINA

Pietro kisses and sucks gently on my clit as my thighs tremble. I'm oversensitized from that incredible orgasm. But he knows every inch of my body, how to build me back up. And he will, over and over before he allows himself to come.

That has always been our rhythm since we were young and new in love and fumbling our way around one another's bodies. But we're grown now, and it's been a long time.

Growling, I roll smoothly onto all fours and grip Alessandro's throat, tossing him down onto the cushion. Thank the gods for vampire females being so strong.

He grunts when I seat myself on his still-hard cock with one quick move. His mouth falls open, scarlet eyes roving my body hungrily. Both hands come to my hips as I glance over my shoulder.

"Come, mate," I command.

Pietro is at my back in a moment, turning my face gently so he can take my lips. His tongue dips into my mouth as Alé's fingers find my clit and pinch. I gasp into the kiss, and Pietro deepens it, fingers curling into my hair.

"Fuck her," Alé pleads, his big hips moving slowly beneath me. He loves it when they take me together. And I agree, it's delicious, so I rub my ass against Pietro's front, marveling at the thickness that nestles between my ass cheeks.

Pietro breaks the kiss and makes a quick slashing motion at his wrist. The first drip of his blood on my back has me arching in pleasure. His sweet but tangy scent fills my senses as he deposits droplets down my back and into my crack. It's a natural lubricant for vampires.

And I want what he's preparing me for.

"Move, Alé," Pietro growls, slipping his fingers down to stroke the tight pucker there. "Bounce her on your fat cock."

Oh gods.

Alé grabs my hips, using his strength to rock me back and forth on his incredible thickness. Every forward motion drags his dick along my G-spot. My eyes roll into my head as I fall forward, planting my hands on his broad chest, hips rocking with his. The beautifully etched tattoos down his neck and over his pecs tell the story of his family. Alé is more highborn than Pietro and me combined, but you'd never know it. His family is cruel and cold. When we were young, he spent all of his free time at my house—or Pietro's.

The steady thrum of his heartbeat calls me. Opening my eyes, I stare at the spot I've longed to bite for so long. Not just bite—claim with my venom.

One day. Denying our bond gets harder by the day. Especially being here with them. It could be like this all the time.

I surge forward and sink my fangs into his pectoral, sucking down big gulps of him. Behind me, Pietro slides a finger, then two, into my ass, stretching and preparing me. But I'm already so full, so ready to combust, my channel pulsing around Alé's hard length.

His blood is the headiest of wines, filling my mouth and dripping down my chin as I suck at the wound. Bloodlust roars through my veins, demanding more of him, more of them.

Mine.

With a snarl, I release the bite and strike again, just above his heart, filling the puncture wounds with my venom. I wanted to bite lower, right into that spot where I could bond him. But I can't do that without a conversation.

We're not ready.

Or are we?

But that thought disappears as Alé bellows his pleasure, gripping the headboard with both hands as his muscles strain and flex. His body is a sculptured gift. Just looking at him gets me hot.

At my back, Pietro slaps my hole with his cock before dragging it between my thighs to brush along Alé's cock. Alé whines as I suck his blood, Pietro lining himself up with my back hole. As he slides in, reverent fingers come to my hair and wrap around it. He reaches around my front and pulls me upright, back to chest. Long, elegant fingers curl around my neck and squeeze.

Alé chuckles beneath me, hands squeezing my thighs. "You've done it now, Valentina. You've unleashed him. Prepare for the maelstrom."

My lips curl into a snarl, but at the first rough snap of Pietro's hips, I nearly come undone. The bond between us jumps and sizzles with pleasure, sending sparks of heat flaring along my skin.

Beneath me, Alé bites his wrist, opening a fresh wound. With a flick of his hand, he splatters blood over my face and chest. I whine as it drips onto my lips, his taste so perfect, so divine.

"More," I demand. "I need more of your beautiful blood, mate."

He rolls his hips hard and slow, driving that delicious cock inside me with measured movements. But at my back, Pietro takes up a fast, steady thrusting motion, my body jerking each time he fills me.

The combination of the two of them has me on sensory overload. I don't know where to focus. Reaching up behind my head, I thread my fingers through Pietro's short hair, holding him close, his breath warm against the side of my face.

"Mate," he growls, his voice ragged with emotion, our bond tight with need. "Mine."

A desperate cry is my answer as I look down at Alé, his mouth dropped open, brows scrunched into a needy vee.

"Yours," I confirm. "Always us."

In that moment, I don't think I can go back to a life without them.

10
ALESSANDRO

I'm barely holding on to my sanity, watching my blood drip down Valentina's beautiful figure. At her back, Pietro ravages her, his hand around her neck squeezing her throat hard as her eyes roll into her head.

It's hard for us both to move in this position, so I remain still, the pace of Pietro's motion enough to drive me wild. With every thrust from him, her channel tightens impossibly around me. It's enough to make me lose my mind, every inch of my body tense and tight and ready to explode a second time. I keep one hand on the headboard, the other teasing her clit as we stretch her.

It's so right between us, despite that missing mate bond between her and me. I've never felt like a third wheel, like I don't belong. And now? When Pietro locks eyes with me over her shoulder…I know I could never belong anywhere else.

He strikes, latching on to her neck, forcing her to milk me harder as I grab at the cushion beneath me and struggle not to spill too fast.

Blood drips in thick ruby rivulets down her breasts and between her thighs, coating us both. She reaches up, placing her delicate hand on Pietro's temple. As if they planned it, they both look down, focusing on me.

"I love you," she whispers. "So much."

And that's when I explode, stars colliding behind my eyelids as bliss erupts, seed spilling from me to fill her.

She clenches around me, falling forward as Pietro pounds into her from behind. They follow me moments later, screaming into the quiet of our playroom.

Bliss fades, my second eyelids retracting. My body is loose, relaxed, sated.

Valentina's lips part, her breathing stuttered as she falls forward on my stomach. Pietro leans over her and grabs my shoulder, rolling us onto our sides with her sandwiched in the middle. I stare at how beautiful they are as he buries his face in her neck, peppering her with tender kisses.

Her beautiful eyes flutter open, and she smiles at me. "I missed you so much, Alé."

I tuck her hair up over her shoulder, giving Pietro better access. His lips trace a bloody path along her skin, sending my cock twitching between us. Watching his tongue lap at trickles of red has my lust building again already.

"Yes, give that to me again." She glances over her shoulder. "Both of you."

And we do. Over and over until she's exhausted from our exceedingly *thorough* attention.

Morning dawns too quickly. I've never been more thankful to have employees who can open Higher Grounds. Every inch of my body aches from last night's vigorous activities.

Eventually, it's time to extricate myself and get ready for my shift downstairs. When I pull away from Valentina, she reaches for me in her sleep, her hand chasing the spot where I lay.

I hit the bathroom for a quick shower. As the water warms, I stare in the mirror. My hair is thoroughly disheveled, my lips swollen and skin spattered with dry blood.

"It was a perfect evening, was it not?" Valentina's throaty voice drifts into the bathroom.

When I turn, she's in the doorway, eyes eating me up.

"Not sated yet?" I question, reaching for her throat.

She grins as I wrap my fingers around her neck and pull her into my arms. When I slant my mouth over hers, she moans into the kiss. Sharp claws come to my chest and scratch hard enough to draw blood.

Groaning at the mix of pleasure and pain, I back us into the shower, spilling water over our bodies. The kiss grows frenzied, but she breaks it with a snarl, dropping to both knees at my feet. My gaze locks onto her red lips as they part, the tip of my cock disappearing into the heat of her soft mouth.

A desperate whine leaves my lips just as Pietro appears in the doorway with a grin. "Watching you together is the ultimate pleasure," he says with a delighted smile. "You're beautiful, both of you."

"Her mouth, mate," I whine. "Fuuuuck…"

Valentina presses forward, groaning around my throbbing length, the vibration tightening my balls. Looking down, I watch hungrily as she pops on and off my cock, sharp fangs teasing my skin when she drags them lightly down my length.

My cheeks heat as Pietro joins us, standing above her as he gets hard. Stroking his cock lightly, he watches her suck me off.

"You could join her," I tease, pointing at my dick.

His grin grows broader. "You liked that, eh? Having me at your feet?"

Valentina smiles, my cockhead brushing along her lower lip. "You know I love it when you touch each other."

I give Pietro a teasing look. "Perhaps you'd like to be standing, and she and I can suck your thick cock while you boss us around."

"Yes," he grits out, jaw tightening as he fists Valentina's hair and guides her mouth to his bobbing dick. He grunts when she closes her lips around it, hollowing her cheeks as she reaches for his sack and cups it, rubbing him.

I drop to my knees, splaying them wide and pulling her into my lap so I can support some of her weight. The shower floor isn't the most comfortable position. But I want to turn her on and make him feel good, so I hold her steady as I lean forward and suckle my way down the side of his cock.

"Fuck, Alé," Pietro grunts. "Take me into your mouth."

Valentina moves to his sack, sucking and nipping as I meet his gaze and open my mouth, taking him a slow inch at a time. His second eyelid flashes over his crimson gaze, big chest heaving until my nose touches his stomach. His dick throbs and flexes in my mouth. Swirling my tongue around him, I suck hard, then swirl again.

"We should do this more often," he commands, his voice ragged.

"I'd love to," I admit.

And I think I know why that is. It's time for all of us to be together, and that means a strengthening of the bond he and I share, too. Along with that will come a more physical draw than we've wished for in the past.

"Maybe you'd like to fuck me one day," I tease. I swirl my tongue around his cockhead as Valentina joins me, her tongue tangling with mine as we fight over who gets to suck his cock.

Playfully, I bite the tip as she dips underneath him and sinks her fangs into my throat. Her venom tightens my muscles as I lock eyes with Pietro. And I know what I see in his intense gaze a moment before he explodes.

He's not going to be able to give her up this time.

And neither will I.

11
PIETRO

I come in moments, focused on my mates as they take what they want. Then I command Alé to hold her up against the wall while they make out. I wash them both, keeping them warm beneath the water as their kisses grow frantic and desperate.

I love it when they connect without me between them. It has never mattered to me that she and I share a fated bond that he doesn't have. He will always be part of us. In fact, we aren't "us" without him. I need her to give him her bond, to pull him into that thread that binds us. I want to feel him with us all the time.

He's never been ready, but I want us to have the conversation before she leaves. I don't think I can let her go again.

Eventually, we can hold the world at bay no longer. We leave the shower, drying her off together as she jokes about how much of a fuss we make over her. Alé gives her one of his soft shirts to wear. We dress her, peppering her with kisses and attention until she reminds us that we have work to do.

And so does she. A stark reminder of what she's technically here for, although I plan to steal her away as much as I can.

This morning, our mate bond is full and happy, tingling pleasantly in my chest. My female is happy, and that is my only goal.

When we leave the loft and head down to the coffee shop, she turns in the doorway and ogles us both. "Let's table the tour for another day. I have some paperwork to do this afternoon. I thought I might bring it here and sit in the corner." Her grin turns wicked. "Will I distract you both too much if I do that?"

"Do it." Alé grasps her throat and runs his thumb over her lower lip. "It will be the most beautiful edging."

"Stay with us tonight," I growl, my voice husky from last night's workout. "Pack your bag and come here."

She winks at us. "Oh, I don't know. The Annabelle is an excellent hostess; perhaps—"

I move with super speed, shoving her carefully to the wall as I pin her with my bigger body. "*I* am an excellent host, mate. Come home to us, or else we'll show up at the inn and do delicious things to you there."

Her smile grows wicked as she heads out of the shop, ignoring a few pointed stares from our patrons.

It's all I can do not to chase after her as she leaves the shop. I'm not even working this morning, but I can't bear to leave Alé's side after last night. I want to be close to him, to talk to him, to make plans for her.

Hours later, I am distracted beyond all belief. Valentina was gone all morning doing…something, but now she sits in the front window at a table with three chairs, jotting something on a small notepad. I wipe the front counter down during a lull between patrons.

Alé comes to my side, clapping me on the back as he leans in close to my ear. "Shall we go tease her, Pietro? I can't stand looking at her and not having my hands on her."

All vampires have excellent hearing. Across the long room, her head snaps up, lips curling into a sensual smile. She sets her pencil down and sashays to the counter, hopping up onto it and planting a tender kiss on the bridge of his nose. She sends mirth and lust into our bond at the same time.

I swing her over the counter. Alé grabs her knee and pulls her legs wide, positioning himself between them. She puts one hand on his stomach and reaches for my hand. "I'll stay with you, but you must take a little time off to play tour guide. There's a lot I need to learn before I leave."

My heart clenches at the word "leave," but I nod. "Anything you need, mate."

Alé slips his hand up her thigh and grips it. "Where would you like to go first?"

She tugs him close by his shirt's lapels but smiles at me. "Well, it would be easier for me to visit the various businesses on my own as I'd like to speak with the proprietors, but I'd really like to see it from above. So…" her voice trails off, and she rubs at the back of one elbow. "Perhaps we could fly tonight?"

Something tender unfurls inside me. My wings ache to come out and shield her from the world. Her wings were never strong enough for her to fly the long distances most vampires are able to. It bothered her in her youth, but I'd hoped, with Alé and me loving her so hard, constantly reminding her how perfect she is, that she would come to see her wings as beautiful in their own right, despite being on the smaller side.

Alé grips her throat and turns her focus to him, his expression more serious than I've seen it in centuries. "We would love to fly with you, amore. Anytime, anywhere."

She smiles, but it's soft and tender, our bond fraught with worry. Her gaze moves to me. "And you'll be there if I can't, you know…" She doesn't say it, but we both know what she's speaking about.

"Always," I confirm, bringing my forehead to hers. "We will always be there for you."

Her smile brightens, and she pulls Alé close to us so we can all hug together. I ignore the hustle and bustle around us as Carolya helps the short line of customers. I'm always diligent with the store, always careful, focused and entirely devoted to Higher Grounds. But with my mates here, together, focus for my business eludes me a little bit.

We breathe the same air, our heads pressed tightly together. But the moment passes, and Valentina slips off the counter and grabs her bag. "I'm headed to the Annabelle to pack my things. How about that flight and a late meal? I can cook for you two for a change."

Alé snorts. "You don't cook, amore; we all know this. Unless perhaps you've learned in the last hundred years."

She plants a hand on her hip. "I absolutely do cook."

"Takeout doesn't count," I tease, watching a pink blush crawl over her cheeks and down her chest.

She opens her mouth to sass me, but the coffee machine behind us sputters. Carolya mutters about the damn machine, and Alé gives me a look.

"We must get to work, amore," he tells Valentina. "Comm us tonight when you're ready."

Alé and I stand like fools, staring as she leaves, hips sashaying sensually. Once she's gone, I force myself to turn to the still-sputtering coffee machine so I can relieve Carolya. My pixie helper slaps a coffee-stained rag on the countertop and gives us a wry look.

"Are you two going to be useless while she's in town?"

"Mhm," Alé confirms cheerfully. "We'll be doing next to no work, friend. Get used to it."

He teases her mercilessly, but, like always, she rolls her eyes and returns to her work with a smile.

I touch her elbow carefully. "We would never leave you stranded in here, Carolya, no matter how distracted we are."

Her smile broadens as she twitches her wings. "We'll see about that, Boss."

Indeed we will, because I am already counting down the minutes to dinner.

12

VALENTINA

Hours later with my packed bag in hand, I ascend the steps to my mates' apartment. But by the time I'm halfway up, Pietro appears in the stairwell, grabbing my bag as he slides a hand to the back of my neck.

The possessive touch shoots my lust sky high, and I turn in the stairwell, shoving him against the wall to take his mouth. He nearly drops the bag as he wraps both muscular arms around me and thrusts his tongue between my lips. As his delicious flavor bursts across my senses, I groan and suck at him, desperate for more.

Our bond snaps, pulls and tightens, demanding more, demanding something deeper. Demanding that *thing* we've never been ready to formalize. Without meaning to, I bring my hand to his chest to cover the stunning *ziol* cross there. He breaks the kiss, blood smeared over his lips, his eyes hooded as he stares at me. In that stare, I see a male who's completely in love, whose focus is me, always me.

"I'm already dreading leaving," I whisper into the space between us.

His lashes flutter, and he tucks my hair behind my ear.

Trailing his fingers down my throat and down into the top of my shirt, he cocks his head to the side.

"We need to talk about that," he says quietly. "Because I don't think I can let you go again. Last time…" his voice trails off as he brings his free hand to his chest. "Alé will tell you I was out of my mind with anguish for months after you left. I would never hold you back from your dreams, but…" He stops speaking, but I know what he means.

"I cried every day for six months," I admit, "last time I went home. It was so terrible. And even though I'm making great career progress, I'm not fulfilled, not like I could be."

His smile is wry. "And yet we cannot give up our dreams, so what are we to do?"

I glance up the stairwell. "Talk with our mate about this. Try to come up with some ideas. I cannot bear the thought of parting from you both again."

"Then let us enjoy each other," he encourages. "The conversation will happen soon enough."

But by the time we reach the top of the stairs, Alé stands there with a thoughtful smile. He's got a dishrag slung over one muscular shoulder, his black button-down open to the waist.

"Damn you look good in that." I wave my hand at all of him.

"I know," he says confidently. "If we're going to have a talk, I want to be half naked or full naked. So, I got started while you two were lurking in the stairwell."

Laughing, I cross the threshold and leap into his arms, taking his mouth as fervently as I took Pietro's. I kiss and kiss and kiss him as Pietro rounds us with my suitcase, disappearing into their apartment.

When we finally part, I call my wings, letting them erupt from my back to flare above my head. Alé's eyes go wide as he takes in the fluttering smoky feathers at my back. Reaching out, he strokes the very edge of my wings, sending heat shooting through me. I love it when he touches my wings. And the way he looks at them, like they aren't lesser, like there's nothing wrong with their smaller size, makes me feel beautiful and cherished.

"I love you." Tears fill my eyes as I think about how much he loves me, how much he's always loved me. "And I want to bite you, Alé."

He calls his wings, flaring them huge and dark up around us, cocooning us in shadows as his lips come to mine. "I want that with a desperation I can't ignore. Let's do it, amore. Let's figure out how to make this work. It's time, my heart."

He's right. It is time, despite my current project and need to succeed. Something has to give.

"We need ideas," I mutter, frustrated because I've always tried to think of ideas for us to be together, and only one thing has ever come to me. That thing is nigh impossible, although I've been considering it for a while.

"We'll figure it out," he says quietly, rubbing his larger wings on mine. "For now, let's fly, mate." He unfurls his wings and tucks them up behind his back.

Pietro reappears in the doorway with a bright smile and a small bag slung over his shoulder. He pats it and beams at me. "Snacks for the flight." He gestures up the hallway. "Let's head for the roof. We can start up there and fly over downtown, then head toward the gas station to give you the full ward experience."

The walls shimmy around us. The building is happy for us, so I pat her gently, careful not to tickle her again.

A door opens at the far end of the hall. Laughing, we grab one another's hands and walk to the door. Ascending a small flight of metal stairs, we reach the top and go out onto the hot roof of the building.

Above us, the haven's protective wards glow faintly green. I call my wings again, and Pietro comes to my front, lifting my chin with one finger.

"We're with you if you want us, alright?" Crimson eyes scan

my face before thin lips pull into a wicked smirk. "You can do this, my love."

Unfurling my wings once more, I reach for my mates' hands. "I know I can do this," I start, "but hang on to me for the first little bit? I still get nervous."

Alessandro steps onto the roof's edge and falls off it, flaring his wings high. He drops from view as I laugh, then he reappears, beating the sky with his beautiful black shadow wings. "Come, amore," he croons. "Jump into the sky, and I will fly below you. Pietro can fly beside you, and we will keep you safe."

Nerves fill my chest, my heart rate spiking as I step to the edge where he floats with no problem.

Pietro wraps an arm around my waist and brings his mouth to my ear, nipping it softly. "I have the utmost faith, mate. Your wings are as beautiful as the rest of you." He slides his hand up between my shoulder blades and then brings the other one to the base of my wings, stroking and touching the shadowy feathers.

Curling forward, I revel in the sensations his stroking elicits —heat, excitement, the need to fly with them. Spreading my smaller wings as wide as they'll go, I step to the very edge and resist the urge to look down three stories to the ground.

Instead, I leap for Alé, beating my wings fast to carry me. I falter and drop, nearly slamming into him, but I manage to catch a current and soar upward. Pietro is a comforting presence next to me as Alé flies upside down with both hands behind his head, winking at me as I claw and grasp at the sky.

I'm like a filly standing for the first time, but when we grab a faster current together, I find my footing and soar easily with my mates.

They guide me up into the clouds, through a series of stronger and stronger currents. Eventually, we're able to grab a current that runs along the underside of the pale green ward. We ride that all the way to the singular country road that humans can access Ever by, if called by the town's magical artifact, a map.

We fly for an hour, until my wings begin to tire. I never fly at Hearth HQ. The last thing I need is Evenia judging my wings and finding my entire personage lacking because of them. I haven't flown in many years.

When I start to flag, dropping out of the sky a few times, Alé comes up underneath me, pulling me to his chest. I cross my arms over his chest, putting my chin on them as I smile at him. He loops and swirls and plays as Pietro flies quietly next to us with a soft smile on his face. Dropping through the clouds, Alé alights gracefully in a field of wildflowers.

Pietro lands next to us and removes the bag from his shoulders. He withdraws a blanket and lays it out flat.

I laugh up at Alé. "You can put me down, mate."

"Can't do it," he says with a chuckle. "I'm still busy feeling you up."

I bury my head in his chest and scent him, listening for his heart and the steady thrum of blood through his veins. "I need to taste you," I say on a sigh. "All over."

"You have the go ahead," Pietro jokes.

Alé drops us gently to the blanket, and Pietro joins us, pressing his big body against mine.

"I packed bruschetta, extra olives, espresso and a little bit of bread." He reaches for the bag. "Oh, and grapes." Grabbing one, he pops it into my mouth, growling when I nip at his fingertips.

Alé finally releases me, but I shove my way between his thighs with my back to his chest. It's so easy with them, so natural to behave like we get to do this all the time.

"Listen," I start, suddenly nervous to share something I've been thinking about for a while. "I want to talk to you both."

Alé's warm lips come to my neck. "Tell me it's about how you're desperate to bite and claim me."

"Well," I chuckle, "that's part of the conversation. But, no. There's something else." Glancing between my handsome mates,

I force a smile despite uncharacteristic nerves and focus on the steady beating of their hearts.

"I've got an idea for a portal station that would connect all the havens together, essentially rendering our current travel methods null." I release my breath, looking between Pietro and Alé.

Their expressions are neutral. I recognize those looks.

Pietro's mouth drops slightly open, crimson eyes scanning my face. "Such a thing has been suggested many times before, has it not?"

"It has," I admit. "Evenia's always shot the idea down because of security concerns. But I've got a couple of ideas bubbling about how we could get around that." I look at Pietro, then over my shoulder to Alé. "How much of a security concern do you feel living here in Ever, versus if you were able to travel to any haven quickly?"

"Give me the option to travel," Pietro gruffs, "to be a tourist and spend money in other havens. The way the portal system is set up now makes it a pain in the ass to visit other parts of the system. We'd see far more travel if there was something like this."

"Agreed," Alé murmurs. "Not to mention you could fuck me every night and go to work every morning at HQ."

"Gods, yes," Pietro moans, shifting onto his knees until he can touch us both. "We need that, mate. Imagine if we could be together all the time. I just, I…"

Words seem to fail him, and I understand it. Time and distance have split us apart for far too long.

"I don't know exactly how it'll work," I admit. "But I am bound and determined to figure it out. The thought of leaving you both is tearing me apart already."

"So, it's time." Alé's eyes tense around the edges. His heart rate speeds up, thumping in his chest as his blood sings for me.

"It's time," I agree. "We've been apart for so long—centuries—

and I can't do it anymore. I don't want to. I want you both with me all of the time. Do you agree?"

Alé pulls me to him, crushing me against his chest as he threads both hands through my hair and hovers his mouth above mine. "Fuck yes, my heart. We need this."

"Agreed," Pietro whispers into my ear, nibbling on the lobe.

"Then, I'll make it happen." The promise falls easily from my lips, as if it's every day I convince Evenia to do something she's refused to do many times.

But more than anything, I believe that now *is* the time for my mates and me to be together. And I will do whatever it takes to make that happen for us.

13
ALESSANDRO

We've never been lucky enough to have Valentina for two full weeks. She keeps busy with research for her project, visiting every single business multiple times and interviewing many of the Evertons. We host a dinner for the haven leadership group in our apartment so she can talk to them about her ideas for the new haven.

They give her tons of excellent feedback, so much so that she finishes her notebook and has to start scribbling in a new one.

It is a marvel watching her work. And it reinforces to me how important her dreams are. She's in her element while haven planning. She's happy.

None of us are any closer to an answer on how to be together when we're fulfilling our dreams so far away from each other. Her idea for the portal station is well thought out, but Evenia isn't known for taking risks. It seems like such a long shot for her to agree to it.

Valentina leaves today. She packed early this morning since it'll take nearly sixteen hours to go through the portals and get back to Hearth HQ.

She and Pietro stand in the doorway kissing. Tears stream

down her face as he strokes her hair with both hands. I watch, helpless to make this better for them, or myself. The familiar ache I get every time she leaves has already taken up residence. I'm hollowed out like a dead, empty tree. I rub at my chest when they break the kiss. She reaches for me and pulls me close, transferring to my arms.

We kiss too, but I'm more desperate than Pietro, devouring her because it's the last time I'll get to do this for who knows how long. A century, maybe.

Or maybe, if her project comes to fruition, we can join her to celebrate the grand opening. Perhaps it won't be so long, after all.

She breaks the kiss first and dabs at her tears. "Okay. I'm going to go. But we have a plan, and if we manifest it enough, it could work."

Pietro and I both nod, but he's already miserable at the idea of her leaving, no matter that we have a *possible* plan.

We manage to make it to the portal station before he goes stoically silent. Valentina turns, slinging her bag over her shoulder, her smile bright but forced.

"I know this seems impossible, but I need you both to trust that I will make this happen for us."

"There's no doubt in my mind," I reassure her, bending to nuzzle and kiss her cheek.

She beams when we part, then flicks her gaze to Pietro. He's silent by my side, and her smile falters. I'd nudge him to respond, but that would be too obvious.

"Of course," he finally manages, his voice ragged with emotion. "You can do this, my love."

She presses into his arms, resting her head on his chest. "I can. I *will*. Because I have to. I can't bear parting another time."

Moments turn to minutes as my mates cling to one another. Eventually, Valentina pulls away from Pietro, adjusting the luggage at her back. "Goodbye, my loves," she whispers.

"Goodbye, amore." I smile despite the ache in my chest.

She gives us a final, watery smile before turning and disappearing into the portal.

The moment she's gone from sight, Pietro begins to tremble, his heart rate spiking.

"Come, mate." I take his hand and guide him back outside. Halfway to the street, he halts and nearly crumples. Holding back my own misery, I gather him in my arms and spread my wings, lifting into the sky. I crawl through the clouds as Pietro stares morosely into the distance. I get us home as fast as I can. We scheduled others to work the shop today, knowing we wouldn't be in a good place after our mate left.

Pietro's head lolls against my forearm as I alight on the rooftop. Carefully, I carry him downstairs and to the kitchen, where I deposit him on our window seat. It's a place he often sits after we've seen her. His face crumples, bloody tears streaking down his light skin as he lets his head fall back against the wall.

He says nothing, but trails of tears become full-on rivers as he sobs.

I run my fingers through my hair, choking on my own grief as I watch him fall apart. I've never known what to do for him when he's like this except be there. Feed him, keep him company, plan the next time we'll get to see her.

But...maybe it's different now. Something changed this time. We all felt more deeply connected, and he and I were more physical than we've ever been. I decide to test something, so I slip behind him in the window seat and pull him between my thighs, resting his head against my shoulder. I kiss the side of his face, his neck and his shoulder. He turns to me, silently asking for more as I lavish my utter adoration on him.

"This is going to work out, mate," I promise him.

It has to. Because it was always meant to be the three of us.

Without her, we're just not complete.

14
VALENTINA

Six months later

The only thing to ease the ache of leaving Alé and Pietro was work. I threw myself into it the moment I got back to Hearth HQ, planning a dozen other trips to the most successful havens in our system. I compiled over fifteen notebooks' worth of notes from those trips, and comm'd my mates every week to tell them what I've been learning and working on.

Like always, Pietro forces brightness into his voice and a smile to his lips, but our bond is dark and quiet. Six portals are too far for me to be able to feel him. If we lived in the human world, it wouldn't be a problem. But six portals plus six ward systems are enough to obliterate it.

It's nearly midnight, and my office is pitch-black save for a solo light on at my desk. I add color to the last illustrated mockup of the new haven. The new haven was announced four months ago, and Evenia uncharacteristically let the Azuroan monsters vote on the name, as many of them will be moving to the new location.

They picked Tesoro, the Italian word for treasure.

I love it. And I hope they'll love what I've planned. I traveled to Azuro last week to speak with the leadership council there and present my final plans. Their signoff is the last step I need before presenting it to Evenia tomorrow for the last approval. Of course, she's given a half dozen approvals along the way. Tomorrow is mostly for show. Typically, it's a public meeting, and anyone can come, but I asked Evenia if we could meet privately.

I'm going to simultaneously present my detailed plan for a Grand Portal Station, much like the humans' Grand Central Station. I haven't spoken a word of this plan to anyone, but I've been working overtime doing research, cost analysis and location planning. I'm ready for this presentation. It has to work; she has to agree, because I can't keep living without my mates like this. Not to mention the benefit to monsterkind.

It's early evening in Ever, so I pick up my comm disk and call them. They don't answer; they're probably busy.

But two hours later, they're still not answering. Worry fills me, so I pack up my things and head home, determined to call them again.

Scurrying down the streets with my plans in a long tube carrier and my bag slung over my back, I push through the snow until I get to my apartment. My chest is full of pressure, and I wish for the millionth time I could ease some of that with my bond.

As I enter my building, I flatten my ears to my head to avoid hearing every conversation in the place. It's a pro and con of being a vampire. But, inadvertently, I pick up voices I'd know anywhere.

Could it be?

I examine my bond only to feel a sensual tug.

In a moment, I fly up the stairs to my apartment on the top level. The front door is propped open. Bursting through, I look for them. Pietro stands at the stove wearing one of my frilly aprons as he stirs a boiling pot, and Alé comes out of the bathroom in nothing but a towel, his black hair wet and dripping water down his powerful neck.

My mouth drops open, but I zip it. Tears fill my eyes. "You're here. You're both here. I was just calling you…"

Alé drops the towel, revealing his nude frame. Like always, his beauty shocks me into silence. Jagged, linear tattoos trail down his neck and cover his chest, a singular line diving all the way into the thick hair around the base of his bobbing cock.

"I need to worship you." I set my tube and bag down on a side table by the door.

"We couldn't wait to see you," Pietro rumbles, removing the apron and hanging it on a hook on the wall. "We took a few days off to be here while you make your presentation. We wanted it to be a surprise."

The first blood tear trails down my cheek as I gesture him close. Pulling them together, I press my cheek to Alé's chest and bring my left palm to Pietro's heart. Instantly, nerves and sadness dissipate. I can do anything with them by my side. Anything at all.

Sighing happily, I consider just how late it is, and yet Pietro seems determined to feed me. I smile and lift my head from Alé's chest, jerking it toward the stove. "You're cooking, so let's eat. After that, would you like to go out on the town for a bit? Or would you rather stay in?"

Pietro bends down and nuzzles my neck. "I wouldn't mind showing you off at a club for a while. It's been years since we went to one."

Alé's hands slide up my back to rest between my shoulder blades. "What do you think?" I question.

His plump lips pull into a smirk. "Can I fuck you while you're tied up?"

"Anytime," I murmur. "We can play however you like."

"Dinner first," Pietro commands, gripping my throat and running his thumb over my lower lip. "We must take care of you first, amore."

"Of course." I kick my shoes off and stride across my sparse apartment, grabbing plates to set the table.

Alé disappears into the bedroom, and Pietro returns to the stove, stirring a saucepan of red sauce, peppers and sausage.

"Smells divine." I wrap my arms around him from behind. His heart thumps steadily under my fingertips. I scent him as he continues cooking. I don't even move, so thankful he's here, until Alé rejoins us with black jeans slung low on his hips. He comes behind me, pulling me from Pietro until my back hits Alé's front.

Bending down, he bites gently along my neck down to my back, pulling my shirt down off my shoulder. Moaning softly, he bites and sucks at my skin, running a hand up between my breasts. "Missed you," he murmurs into my skin. "Six months was terrible, amore."

"I know," I manage, letting my head fall to one side as my bond with Pietro tenses, flush with need and pleasure. "Six months felt like a century."

Pietro turns, eyes flashing as he watches Alé nip his way back down my neck and along my skin. "We cannot do the distance anymore, my love. Whatever Alé and I have to give up, we are prepared to do it. We need you."

"No," I growl. "I won't let you give up your dreams. I *will* convince Evenia to approve the Grand Portal Station plans."

"It's not that we don't have faith in you," Alé whispers against my neck. "It's that we are planners, and our backup plan is to come here no matter what."

"I hate that plan." I pull Pietro close. "I need things to work out for all of us."

"They will," Pietro says quietly. "If anyone can pull this off, it's you."

"I need your bite," Alé moans, moving to the other side of my neck. "Now, Valentina. Please."

I've never heard his voice so ragged and raw, so desperate. My bond with Pietro tenses and flexes. He wants this too.

And so do I. I've wanted it for centuries.

I turn in Alé's arms. His eyes are hooded, expression somber when he brings his scarlet gaze to mine.

I reach up and run my fingers along his strong jawline. "I'm ready, mate. Where do you want to be?"

"Right here, right now," he demands roughly, bringing one hand to my hair and gripping it tightly. He looks to his right. "Be with me?"

Pietro joins us, sliding a hand around Alé's waist. He moves his other hand to the back of my neck as nerves flare through me.

I'm going to bite Alé—finally. A vampiric claiming bite is an ancient bit of evolutionary magic from a time when vampires were hunted. So many lost their mates that we developed the ability to bond any being to us through a bite filled with venom and intention. I've bitten Alé a trillion times, but never with the intent to bind his soul to mine and Pietro's. Pietro could bite Alé and do the same thing. But, somehow, we always knew it would be me who did it.

Baring my fangs, I lean down and lick a path over Alé's heart. It's beating so fast, like a wounded sparrow trapped behind his bones, aching to be released.

"Alé," I look up at him, "I love you."

As he opens his mouth to respond, I strike, sinking my fangs deep into the chest muscle over his heart. He gasps, fingers tightening in my hair as Pietro stands quietly with us, safeguarding us.

I pour centuries of love into the bite, claiming him with every bit of my soul as I fill his heart with my venom. I don't drink him —no, this is about giving. I fill him as his hips begin to rock against mine, his soft grunts becoming full-on pants until they rise and he comes with a guttural roar.

Something bright snaps and twists between us.

Our bond. The one we've wanted for centuries.

It spins and braids itself along the gleaming tension Pietro and I share until I can't tell where either bond starts or ends. Alé's head falls back against the wall, his throat bobbing as I release the bite and stare in awe at him. His feelings are exactly what I always thought they'd be—joyful adoration, cheerful confidence, and a deep, undying loyalty to Pietro and me.

It surprises me when Pietro leans into Alé and sinks his fangs into our mate's throat. He drinks deeply, groaning with need as Alé whines and holds me closer. Through the bond, their pleasure and desire are tangible. I love that they've become more physical in the last six months or so. I never thought they'd want that, but it's beautiful to see their love blossom and deepen in this way.

Alé comes again from the bliss of Pietro's fangs, and I watch, because they're mine now, irrevocably. As Pietro releases the bite and pulls away, resolve fills me.

I'll crush this presentation tomorrow. I have to. Because I can never, ever allow my males to give up a single one of their dreams. Not for me. Not for anything.

15
ALESSANDRO

She bound me. She *bound* me. Something I've wanted since we were teens all those centuries ago. Something I've wanted with a depthless aching need that none of our visits ever alleviated.

The last six months of misery dissipate, gone on the wind as her and Pietro's love fills me. I marvel at being able to feel their emotions in my chest. Pietro's thinking dark things about fucking us. She's overwhelmed and thrilled at feeling me.

And me? I'm home. It doesn't matter where we go; as long as they're with me, I'll be happy.

Valentina looks at me, adoration obvious in the softness at the corners of her beautiful ruby eyes. "I'm going to change into something sexier. Then let's grab a drink and go to the club, assuming you still want to go?"

It's on the tip of my tongue to say no, let's stay home and fuck. But we can go fuck in front of others, flaunting our bond. And I love to show her off.

"Wear something see-through," I encourage, slapping her ass.

"Done," she croons, reaching down to give Pietro's hard-on a squeeze before she sashays out of the room.

When she goes, he bends forward and nuzzles the tip of my nose with his. "I love feeling you in here." He brings my hand inside his low-cut shirt to his heart before his lips brush mine. "I can't wait to feel you in here while we fuck her."

Heat flares through me. I love this new dynamic between us, feeling his emotions threaded through mine.

"I want it." I brush my lips to his. "I've wanted it for a long time, Pietro."

He opens his mouth to say something, but Valentina emerges from her room in a sheer lace top and black leather miniskirt. Every dip and swell of her body are visible to us, from peaked red nipples to that firm stomach I love to bite.

"What do you think?" She holds her arms out and spins.

My breath halts in my chest. "Stunning," I manage. But "stunning" isn't an adequate enough word to describe how hauntingly beautiful she is. And it was always like that for me, despite that missing bond.

She puts a hand on her hip, sticking it out. "Well, you two look appropriately gobsmacked, and I feel like a goddess, so shall we go?"

"Yeah," I manage like an idiot, wiping my hand over my mouth. "Or what if—"

"We're going," Pietro demands, grabbing my shoulders and shoving me toward the door. If we decide we'd rather be home, we'll come back.

Ten minutes later, I'm glad he kicked my ass out the door. We stand in front of a building designed to look like a human cathedral, although nothing holy is happening inside. The entire place smells like blood and fucking. An arched gothic door is painted the same black as nearly everything in this haven.

A tiny door opens at eye level, and a red iris appears. The vampire looks at Pietro and me before growling, "Password?"

Valentina pushes between us and laughs. "Password? Come on, Yaitzen, let us in."

The tiny door slams shut, and Valentina grabs my hand. Moments later, locks click and retract, and a big vampire male opens the door for us. The moment he lets us through, he shuts it and locks it once more.

We say nothing as he gives us wristbands, but I don't miss the hungry look in his eyes when Valentina offers her wrist. I suppose it's possible he's tasted her at some point or another. She probably frequents this place. But I don't give a fuck because tonight she's here with us.

We silently follow her down a long dark hallway and into the cavernous main room. Dancers hang in cages from the ceiling, dripping bags of blood onto the throng below. Stained glass windows line the entire space all the way to an altar at the front where a giant centaur fucks a vampire female strapped to a mounting table.

My balls tighten and fill at the orgy on the floor below us. Different scenes are laid out, each one surrounded by a throng of onlookers either waiting their turn or just there to watch. If this is like other clubs, there'll be a number of rooms in the back dedicated to specific scenes like forest chases and the like.

"Where do you want to start?" Pietro rubs the backs of his knuckles along Valentina's jawline.

"I want the mounting stand," she says, fangs flashing.

I laugh and run a hand through my hair. "Go big or go home?"

"Exactly," she purrs, starting down the stairs.

We pass a dozen scenes I'd be thrilled to stop at, but when we reach the altar, excitement riles me. She was right to pick this. It's so impossibly hot, I can barely stand it.

Attendants for the scene gather a sweating, gasping vampire female and carefully remove her from the stand. When they take her off, a river of creamy cum drips from her well-used pussy. Her head lolls back as they carry her off stage and down a dark hallway to rest.

I've only seen a centaur scene like this once, when we were teens and snuck into a club back home, but it stuck with me.

Valentina spins and places a hand flat on each of our chests. "I live here, so I can come any time. Is there anything you'd rather do than this particular scene?" She jerks her head toward the centaur, who's watching as another female, a minotaur, ascends the altar and leans over the cylindrical mounting table. He bends down and flips her miniskirt up around her waist, kneeling so he can bury his nose between her ass cheeks.

"Nope," I pop. "This is it."

Pietro grins and grips her throat, pulling her closer to him until his lips brush over hers. "This is perfect, Valentina."

They start making out, and I watch for a few minutes. The grunting of the minotaur female grabs my attention. She grips the round mount, riding it as the centaur male dwarfs her, fucking her hard and deep. He's massive, and I'm having a hard time imagining him and Valentina fitting.

An attendant moves toward us, drawing my gaze. He taps Valentina and leans into her ear. "You want the potion to take him?"

Her eyes flash white as the second lid covers them. "Yeah." She's breathless, expectant, excited.

The attendant hands her a small bottle filled with green liquid. In a flash, she winks at me and unstoppers it, downing it in one gulp.

I reach down and adjust my cock, grinning as I think about her taking all of that male up on the stage. The potion will make it possible for her to do so. It's a unique concoction created by vampires for vampires. I have no idea *what* other species of monster do if they wanna fuck this guy.

Before long, it's our turn. The minotaur female stumbles off the stage into the waiting arms of two helpers. Valentina gracefully ascends it and stops before the centaur. He stands, cock erect and dripping. He's handsome, his horse half covered in a shiny white hide. His human half is sun-kissed and golden. Long blond waves fall around his shoulders. He's a warrior, though, based on the scars that crisscross his chest, stomach, and arms.

Something about that heats me up. My perfect little delicate woman getting railed by this giant beast of a male.

He reaches for her shirt and slips it off her shoulders. Pietro comes to my side and reaches down, palming my cock.

"I need to be up there," I mutter. Grabbing his hand, I drag him up the six steps to the platform where the mounting bench is. The centaur doesn't bother to look at us as he pulls her shirt off and tosses it aside.

I stand beside the bench, facing the crowd, with Pietro at my back.

Valentina's hands come to her skirt, shoving it down, but the centaur stays her hand. "Leave that on," he commands.

She throws her glossy hair over her shoulder and waits for him to make the first move. He steps forward, reaching down to pull her up into his arms. Her legs go around his waist as he clip-clops to the mounting bench and sets her down on it.

Someone in the crowd mutters, and I twitch my ear to hear what they're saying.

"Get on with it!" another male shouts.

My mate is a tease, and this centaur knows how to work a crowd.

He pushes her skirt up. Dark eyes flick to hers. "Show me everything, pretty girl."

Valentina rocks back onto her elbows, bringing one foot flat on the mounting bench, drawing the centaur's hungry gaze to the juncture of her thighs. I risk a glance at the audience. Most are openly stroking themselves or being fucked as they watch her. I reach for Pietro and palm his cock. He's hard. I bet he aches like I do.

The centaur drops to his forelegs so his human half is nestled between her thighs. Dipping even lower, he brings his nose to the inside of her knee and chuffs. He scents her all the way to her pussy, where he groans softly. Bringing one hand to her belly, he presses her flat on the bench. He curls his other arm around her propped-up knee, holding the top of her inner thigh and spreading her wide.

When he licks a hard, hot path up her pussy and over her clit, she arches on the bench, white eyelid flashing over her ruby eyes.

Pietro presses against me. His hips begin to rock as I slide my hand into his pants and grip his shaft at the base. Valentina cries out, reaching one hand up behind her head, fingers curling as she reaches for us. Pietro strokes two fingers along her palm, to the tip of each finger as the centaur eats her with increasing roughness.

The crowd around us is intoxicating, the scents of blood and pleasure combining into a maelstrom of bliss as orgasm overtakes my pretty little mate. Her screams mesh with the rising crowd and the desperate, huffy grunts of the centaur as his rhythm goes jagged and wild.

I can't move my eyes from his big flat tongue and scarred lips. Our new bond is awash with pleasure that's practically a physical touch. Jerking Pietro hard, I pant in his ear as orgasm swirls and eddies in my balls, not quite close enough, but threatening to surprise me out of nowhere.

The centaur rises, guiding Valentina's leg off one side of the bench. Her chest heaves, nipples pebbled to sharp points as he steps between her thighs and strokes her pussy with a practiced touch. He leans down, big upper body resting lightly on hers as he brings his mouth to her ear, stroking sweaty hair away from her forehead.

I marvel at the scent of her pleasure mixed with his deep pine essence.

"I'm going to fuck you now," he murmurs, "and it's going to feel so good, but if it's ever too much, say 'red.' Nod if you understand."

Valentina smirks and nods, turning her head to the left so her lips nearly brush his. He stiffens, but she waits, not forcing any further touch from him. He seems to marvel at her clear offer of a kiss, and after a moment where his eyes move hungrily over her face, he closes them and presses his mouth to hers.

The crowd screams with need, but he ignores everything as he kisses my mate, their tongues tangling together, the kiss desperately sensual. He plunders her mouth with a warrior's efficiency, taking and taking as Valentina's scent blooms from his attention.

When they part, he looks thoughtful.

Everyone loves Valentina. It's easy to see. She enraptures *everybody*.

But she's all mine.

16
PIETRO

Alé's big hand strokes to the tip of my cock and squeezes, sending heat spearing through my core and down my spine.

The centaur glances over at us for the first time and jerks his head. "Step back a bit."

We shuffle backward, although Alé never stops tugging my dick. Instead, he encourages me to rest my weight against him as he holds me up and jacks me off. It feels too good, and I groan. But then the centaur bunches his weight to his hindquarters. He lurches forward and rises high above the mounting block, his cock bobbing close to Valentina's pussy.

He rests his forefeet on two wooden blocks to keep his weight off her as an attendant joins us on the altar. Fascinated, I stare at the way he positions himself as I unzip my pants and place my hand over Alé's while he jacks me with slow, hard strokes.

The centaur closes his eyes, head falling back as the attendant grabs his bobbing cock and guides it between Valentina's thighs. She gasps as he nudges into her, back arching as she reaches above her head to clutch two handles sewn into the leather bench. His mouth drops open as he arches his back, his cock filling her so full, the tip is visible through the taut skin over her belly.

"That's so fucking hot," Alé grinds out, his grip on my cock growing hard to the point of pain. "Look how big his dick is, filling our pretty little woman. Think she loves it?"

I can't find an answer as precum spurts from me in hot jerks.

The centaur teases in and out of our mate until he's seated fully inside her, his dick visibly twitching and flexing inside her body. He lets out a soft, worshipful noise, running both hands through his long hair before pulling out of her. From his position, he can't see her buried under the horse half of his figure, so I wonder what he's thinking about as he fucks her?

Then Alé reaches down and slides two fingers behind my sack, playing with the sensitive skin there as he brings his free hand to my shaft.

"I want to suck you off," he growls into my ear. "But I don't want to miss a second of this."

"I want to bite her and you," I admit, "but I can't reach her." I remove his hands from my pants and grab his jeans, hauling him in front of me. Yanking his shirt off his shoulders, I revel at popping buttons and tearing fabric before sinking my fangs into the spot where his neck and shoulder meet.

When I pierce a vein and suck, he groans, grinding his ass against my throbbing, aching cock. In front of us, the centaur rhythmically fucks Valentina, whose body jerks and writhes on the bench as he builds her pleasure.

Alé grunts, letting his head fall to one side as blood dribbles down the front and back of his neck. I release the bite and lap at it before biting another place and another and another. It's so damn hot, watching that big dick saw in and out of her, pressing against her from the inside out. Knowing he's hitting her G-spot with every thrust has me ready to explode.

My mate groans, his tone needy and low as I find another spot under his ear and sink my fangs in again. He reaches down and pulls his cock out, jerking it with both hands while I suck his blood.

The bond with Valentina is tense with pleasure. She's so close to coming, focused on that enormous dick and sending love to us all at the same time.

My body tenses as Alé's breathing goes shuttered and halting. He's about to explode. I infuse my venom into the bite, and he jerks, crying out as his muscles flex and pop. As he comes on a keening cry, Valentina looks over at us, eyes rolled into the back of her head, although she tries to focus. She snarls watching Alé, and then a giant swell of lustful bliss fills our bond, crashing through her in a wave of pleasure so intense, it sparks my orgasm, and I spurt hot seed all over Alé's back, roaring into the bite.

Sound muffles, and my vision blurs, white eyelids flashing over my eyes as everything narrows down to my mates and the sheer pleasure coursing through us. More seed shoots down my shaft, coating Alé's skin as orgasm tears through me like a train.

Moments turn to a minute, maybe longer before ecstasy fades, and I'm left trembling, breathing hard into my mate's neck. The centaur still thrusts slowly in and out of Valentina, seed dripping from her like a leaky faucet. The ground beneath the bench is covered in cum. She made him come too—hard, from the looks of it.

He pulls out of her but shimmies enough to bring his cock to rest on top of her clit. A few more hard thrusts drag his enormous length along her most sensitive spots. He groans and closes his eyes as I wrap a hand around Alé's torso, gripping his throat. His heart races, delicious blood coursing through his veins from the orgasm and watching our mate be taken so deeply.

An attendant appears on the other side of the centaur, clearing his throat and speaking low. "We have more guests, sir. Can we wrap this up?"

The centaur's lips curl back into a snarl, but eventually, he sighs and crawls carefully off the mounting block.

Alé and I stand fascinated, watching the process. I don't need attendants to help my woman off the mounting table, but I sense in our bond that she isn't done.

Covered in sweat, nipples still pebbled, she sits up and shifts onto her knees, rising so she's nearly at face height with the centaur. She reaches up and strokes the backs of her knuckles along his jawline. The male's pale lashes flutter against his skin as he closes his eyes and sinks into her touch.

Heat swirls through me, pleasure building again at how fucking sensual she is. A goddess among vampires. Alé moans.

Valentina smiles at the enormous male. "That was absolutely lovely. Thank you for the gift of your pleasure."

He takes her hand and turns it over enough to kiss her palm, never looking away from her. "Find me any time, little one. That was...exceptional."

The idea of her coming here to be fucked by him some other time makes me want to never leave. I want to see every orgasm she ever has. I want to watch her tease him in other ways. I want to come back and do this again and again.

Valentina rises to a stand and leans forward, pressing her plump lips to the centaur's cheek. He tenses, surprised, but then softens into her touch. A quick tug at our bond tells me she's ready to go. I push Alé forward, and he understands, crossing the altar with his pants half off to swoop Valentina into his arms. I reach down and pull his pants up as she tucks her head beneath Alé's chin and hums happily.

Ruby eyes come to mine. "What else do you want to do, mate? There are endless possibilities."

"Home," I grit out, realizing I want to be in our bed. I look up at Alé.

He smiles. "I will never complain about being home in our bed. Let's go."

I gather our discarded clothing, dipping my head at the centaur as I descend the altar. His pale eyes follow me as I leave his scene.

Meeting my mates at the entryway, I hand them their clothing so we can redress to go outside. The weather here is distinctly colder than Ever, and while I love it, I don't want my cock exposed to it.

It seems like mere minutes pass until we're back at Valentina's small apartment. It's small but cozy, and not as sparse as I'd have thought for a workaholic. Opening the door for Alé, who insisted on carrying her all the way home, I scent the air. So much sex and blood. It's delicious, and I'm ready for more, but my mate is asleep in Alé's arms.

He casts me a quick glance as he sails through the door. "Think she'll want a quick bath?"

I return the look. "Or do you want to lick centaur cum from her pussy to wake her up? Because I think I want to do that…"

His second eyelid flashes over his eyes. "That," he grits out breathlessly. "I want that."

Valentina doesn't stir when we reach the bedroom and Alé sets her carefully down on the bed, nestled in the middle among silken sheets. A giant window takes up the whole back wall of her bedroom, giving us a beautiful view of a snowy midnight sky.

After shedding my clothes, I dip onto the bed and reach beneath Valentina, tugging the corset off her.

"Leave the skirt," Alé commands. "That skirt is fucking hot."

"Agreed," I murmur, running a hand up her cum-covered thigh to reveal her pussy.

Alé joins me, sniffing the air as we lean in close to examine her. Her pussy lips are pink and swollen, covered in creamy white cum and looking so perfectly used. My balls fill painfully. I need to come again, and there's nothing like oral to get me primed. Dipping low, I slick my tongue up her channel, swirling the tip around her clit.

Valentina moans softly but doesn't wake. I know from centuries of experience, though, that she loves to be woken with oral. So I growl softly into her pussy and lick again.

"Lift her ass," Alé demands. "I need space."

Sliding both hands under her ass, I prop her up and focus on spearing her channel with my tongue. The taste of the centaur's cum mixed with her bliss has me thrusting against the bed for friction. Alé moves to her opposite side and brings his mouth down over her clit, hollowing his cheeks as he sucks.

Heady need fills our bond as she wakes and moans, taking in the sight of us.

"More," she commands. "Harder."

I reach down and use the sticky centaur cum to play with her ass until I can get two fingers in. Stretching and thrusting, I continue lapping at her channel as Alé sucks and licks at her clit. She grunts and arches, her body asking for more until Alé and I are in a near frenzy, eating her with rough, hard strokes.

Valentina's muscles begin to tremble, her movements going jerky as her cries go louder, more desperate. Alé cries out, flicking her clit with the tip of his tongue as I finger her ass. When she explodes, she squirts, covering us both in her pleasure as orgasm racks her body hard. She claws at the sheets and screams our names over and over, desperate pleasure yanking our bond tight.

It's a near physical tug on my sack, which fills as my cock bobs against my thigh. I need to come again, hard and inside my woman.

The moment her orgasm fades, I slap her ass, filling my hand with as much as I can grab. She yips and snarls, glancing down at me, eyes flashing with desire.

"Get on top of him," I command.

Alé flops to his back and reaches for her, pulling her to straddle his cock. In a swift move, he guides himself into her pussy and lets out a guttural groan.

"Fuck, Pietro, she's so godsdamned wet."

I run a hand up her spine to grip her neck, bringing my chest to her back. "I'm going to slide inside you with our mate," I murmur into her ear as her head lolls against me. "I want to feel his cock pulse and throb when he comes. We're going to fill you like that centaur did. I want you dripping with *our* pleasure, understand?"

"Yes," she moans.

We've taken her like this before, but being in her pussy together requires plenty of prepwork given our relative sizes. But since she took the potion for the centaur, she'll be ready for us fast.

Alé knows what to do, so he brings his legs close together so that I can straddle them. Then he pulls her forward so her breasts smash against his stomach. He chases her mouth with his lips, kissing deeply as I stare at his cock inside her sweet pussy.

I can't resist. Reaching down, I palm his sack and stroke the part of his cock that's not inside her. He grunts and parts from her, groaning. I had intended to thrust into her immediately, but the sight of them connecting is too much. Bending all the way down, I lick a stripe up the base of his cock, all the way to her pussy, which gets a luxurious lick up and down. Their breathy sighs and soft grunts add fuel to the fire burning in my core. I go wild, biting and kissing and licking as Alé's hips move. His hands come to Valentina's upper thighs, and he rocks her with him, fucking into her.

I watch, fascinated as he pulls her nearly off him and then slams back inside, his thrusts going hard and deep. Gripping the base of his cock, I pull it toward me so she sits just above it. In a swift move, I swallow him whole, loving the way he jerks up to meet the heat of my mouth.

This new thing we're doing where he and I enjoy one another is intoxicating. Through our new bond, his shock and pleasure stroke me. I lap at his slit, wrapped in his scent, her scent, and the centaur's cum. It's a delicious concoction I can't get enough of.

Valentina shifts forward, showing me her gorgeous pussy as she kisses Alé, murmuring in his ear how deeply she loves him, how she'll never let him go, how he's always been hers.

Popping off his cock, I surge forward and bury my tongue in her pussy, her words faltering. I eat her until I can't take it, and then I return to his cock and deep throat his length, growling as I release him from my mouth.

"Stop playing," he growls, the rare command from him to me in the bedroom.

Rubbing his cockhead, I lick a few more times before guiding it back inside our mate. They both cry out as he sinks deep inside her. I debate if I want her ass or her pussy, but decide I need to feel him. Her pussy is perfection, but adding the feel of my dick rubbing against his is…heaven.

Sitting upright, I bring one hand to her hip and the other to the base of my cock. I slap her ass with it, her soft skin rubbing mine. Dragging my cock up the base of Alé's, up and through her pussy lips, I tease them until she spits and hisses like a cat, glaring at me over her shoulder.

She's needy in our bond, ready for us both, wanting more than this playful thing I'm doing.

Reaching down, I grip her ass cheeks and slide my thumbs inside her pussy, admiring her pink, cum-filled channel. Spreading her a little wider, I make a spot and notch my cockhead into it. Moving my hips carefully, I pant as the tip of my dick disappears into her, rubbing Alé as I go.

He grunts out a string of expletives as she sighs and falls fully forward on his chest. Burying her face in his neck, she nips her way along the strong column as I push deeper inside. The feel of my dick rubbing against his shaft is nearly enough to make me come. He's so hot and hard and soaking wet. But her pussy clenched tightly around us is deliciously tight.

Gritting my teeth against the heat that streaks down my spine, I stare at where we're both inside her.

And then I move.

With every drag of my dick out and thrust back in, Valentina tightens around us. Alé holds her hips tightly, fingers curled into her soft skin as centaur cum coats us both, wet, sloppy sounds ringing into the bedroom.

Lightning bolts zip to my sack as cum builds and heat eddies between my legs. I'm on the knife's edge of losing my mind, every touch of Alé's cock driving me insane. And every time I thrust inside her, it pushes Alé against her G-spot.

Valentina pushes upright, changing the angle of our fucking as she tries to rock her hips. "Harder," she growls. "I need you wild, mate."

She doesn't have to tell me twice. Placing my hand just above Alé's on one of her hips and gripping her neck with the other, I punish her sweet pussy, my cock a battering ram shunting in and out of her with thrusts so hard, she nearly falls off Alé with every pass.

But our woman loves it rough, so I infuse my darkly dominant need into every punch of my hips until she's screaming and strangling our cocks. Alé falls with her, bucking and groaning and gripping the headboard like he's dying.

Orgasm hits me watching them, and I go wild, rhythm erratic as I fuck her like it's the last time I'll ever get a chance to, like I'm branding her pussy with my cock.

Over. And over. And over.

Hours later, Valentina's curled around a pillow in bed. I sit in the window seat in her kitchen, staring out over the dark city. The falling snow is peaceful.

"I can see why she likes it here," Alé says quietly, padding through the kitchen to join me. He sits gracefully opposite me, pulling one leg up to rest his arm on it as he looks out the window. After a few quiet moments, he looks at me. "I have all the faith in her, but you know I like a backup plan. Would you want to come here and start over if Evenia doesn't agree to the portal station? I assume so, based on our earlier conversation."

I sigh. This has always been the crux of our problem. None of us have ever wanted to be forced to give up our dreams. We've always hoped and prayed it would work out in the end.

Eventually, I shake my head. "We need another path, Pietro. We're happy in Ever. She's happy here. But…"

"I know." His tone is soft, thoughtful. "It'll crush me if she's not successful. I'm on board with moving here if Evenia doesn't approve the plan. I know it's not what we want, but perhaps it could be short-term. Or we could split our time somehow."

We've considered all of these options over the years.

"I don't know if she'd let us," I say with a huffy laugh. "She's always been so adamant about us not giving up a single dream for her. Since we were young, we've always said that."

"We wouldn't do it without further conversation, obviously," he says. "But I don't think I can do this anymore. And now that I feel her in my chest, it'll kill me when we leave…"

Focusing inwardly, I look for her like I've done for centuries. But this time, she's there. Peaceful and safe and dreaming of something sweet. When we part from her, it'll crush me, and I'll feel her and Alé's pain as well.

"You're right," I concede. "I'm going to assume she'll be successful, because I believe, if anyone can be, it's Val. But…" I trail off as I stare at my handsome mate. "If she's not, we should tell her we'd like to come here, for real. We mentioned it earlier, but we should revisit it."

Alé says nothing, eyes glittering in the darkness. But I sense his agreement and resignation in our bond. He doesn't love that plan, and he doesn't think she'll love it either, but he believes it's the right thing to do.

And when it comes to Valentina's happiness, we will always choose that.

17
VALENTINA

Nerves bash around my insides as I pace across the dark stone lobby of Hearth HQ. The friendly minotaur security guard smiles at me and nods, big, powerful horns dipping respectfully.

He doesn't know I have my huge presentation today, but it feels like he's giving me a little boost when he smiles and examines my briefcase and storage tube. I almost hiss at him to be careful when he pokes around at my mockups. I hold my tongue, though.

The bond in my chest warms and glows with confidence. Alé and Pietro fill me with love from the inside out, and that love pushes some of the nerves away. I wish they could be with me for the presentation, but I'd already asked Evenia to do this privately. If I know anything about my prickly boss, it's that surprising her with Grand Portal Station in a room full of our coworkers would *not* go well.

Once the security guard's done with his investigation of my things, I cross to the elevators and step through a sparkly blue surface to detect any spells or potions. It's something Evenia's always insisted on. She allows no magic inside Hearth HQ aside from the building being alive like they all are.

That done, I rush to the elevator and ride it to the top floor where her office is, examining myself in the shiny interior paneling. Kohl lines my eyes, darkening them and lending me a somewhat vicious air. I've pulled my long waves high onto my head in a tight, efficient bun. I dressed in a fitted gray skirt and vest with a matching collared shirt that dips low, showing my family tattoos.

Evenia loves a strong look, and I'm counting on that to get me off to a good start.

When the elevator doors open into a shiny black waiting room, I wear a confident smile. Heels clacking on the stone floor, I cross a sumptuously decorated midnight lobby to a desk where Evenia's executive assistant sits.

"Hello, Aberen," I croon to the handsome vampire seated there. "I'm here for my ten a.m. presentation."

The elegant, ancient vampire, who's also one of Evenia's two mates, dips his head at me. "I'll let her know you're here. Have a seat, please; we're running a few minutes behind."

No the fuck she's not, I want to scream. It's a power play. She always lets me stew for a solid ten minutes before she allows me into her office. I've been her direct report for almost two hundred years. I'm well aware of her tactics.

Instead, I smile and nod, then turn and cross the lobby. I drop into one of the tufted black velvet chairs and set my bag and tube next to me.

Half a fucking hour later, Evenia's office doors swing open, and she steps gracefully out, giving me a hard once-over. Her other mate, Betmal, steps out with a sour look on his face and a stack of paperwork tucked under one arm.

He doesn't say a word to her or Aberen as he lifts his chin and heads for the door. I know better than to even look his direction or act like something's wrong. But the air smells irritated and sour as she waves for me to enter her office.

When I do, she slams the door behind us. Ominous worry fills me. If she was arguing with her mate prior to this meeting, we might not get off to a good start.

"Evenia," I begin, "we can do this another time if—"

"Did I say it was a bad time?" she snaps, waving at the empty office. Like outside, everything is dark and elegant. Plush black rug, black velvet drapes, even her desk is glossy black wood, inlaid with her family crest.

There's no good answer to her question, so I don't answer it, assuming it's more rhetorical than anything. I set my bag down on an inky velvet chair in front of her desk, withdrawing my proposal book, my art stand, and a pen and blank notebook for any feedback.

She rounds the desk and sits, crossing one leg slowly over the other with her eyes narrowed. I won't let her ruffle me and fuck this up, so I quickly set up the stand and attach my illustrated mockups to the top. They're in order. I'm ready for anything she throws at me.

I send love to my mates, and then I shut down any focus on the bond while I do this. I need this to work—for them, for me, for all the monsters this is a pain point for now.

Leaning forward, I slide my proposal notebook across the shiny desk to Evenia. Nodding at it, I meet her gaze. "Within my proposal, you'll find all the information you asked for, including a layout of the suggested area for the new haven, as well as all the schematics of the main living area. I've aggregated feedback from our top six performing havens in terms of growth and happiness. It's all there. For today, I thought it might be easier to walk through mockups of Tesoro, a name voted on systemwide by our constituents. But if you'd prefer to walk through the proposal itself, we can do that too."

She eyes the proposal book but doesn't reach for it. Instead she brings a finger to her chin as her gaze flicks to the mockups. "Start there. I'll tell you if we need to pivot."

"Excellent," I croon, stepping to the mockup.

The cover art is beautiful and took me ages.

"Welcome to Tesoro," I say confidently, "the haven system's newest addition."

For the next hour, I walk her through every mockup. They detail everything from access to the haven for any humans called by Tesoro's yet-to-be-determined magical artifact, to the school system, to the design of the downtown and separate areas for different types of monsters.

Evenia says next to nothing until I reach the final page, a gorgeous illustration of a statue featuring Evenia and her mates. Her eyes flash when I get to that. Worry fills me, based on the look on Betmal's face when he left her office. But, if anything, her gaze softens slightly.

"Laying it on a little thick, aren't you?" Her tone is brusque, but I sense a tender undercurrent.

"Well," I shrug as I smile, "in our network of over fifty havens, there's not a single building or statue dedicated to the architect of our system. I don't believe you've ever asked for one, but I thought it might be time for us to show you our appreciation for the home you created for us."

That's only partially true. I took Betmal to lunch last week and asked him how to nail this presentation. The statue was his idea.

She rises and rounds the desk, staring at the statue. "I hate this outfit," she barks. "We'll have to find something else that makes me look less sensual and more…powerful." Red eyes flick to mine. "I trust that won't be an issue."

"It can be anything you want," I confirm. Shooting her a wink, I laugh. "Admittedly, I picked this outfit because I'm always jealous when you wear it. It makes your ass look great."

Nobody else could get away with this level of sass. Nobody. But I've learned when and how I can push her.

She snorts and crosses her arms, leaning against the desk. Her smile is thin, but it's there. "Obviously, I haven't read the formal report, but this is very promising, Valentina. Well done."

Pride fills me, and I inadvertently push it to my mates, who cautiously send their love back. I resist the urge to rub at my chest. It's too early to celebrate.

"There's actually something more," I admit, "something that's been a passion project of mine that I'd love for you to consider."

She cocks her head to the side, looking precisely like the predator she is. "Oh, Little Dove?"

Before I can lose my nerve, I pull a second stack of mockups from the storage tube. Tacking them over the first series, I resist the urge to see what expression she wears.

I run my fingers over the blank page on top, focusing on Evenia. "One thing I heard consistently in my research, and that we've heard in every survey we've sent about the haven system, is that inter-haven travel is a challenge."

"We can't fix that," Evenia says in a tone that brooks no challenge. "It's necessary for the safety of the system."

"I've got a unique proposal for that," I counter, lifting the first page.

Evenia's eyes narrow at the illustration, but I barrel on, determined to show her what my idea consists of.

"This is Grand Portal Station." I point to an illustrated great room with glowing green portal doors around the entire perimeter of the oval. Glancing at her, I force a smile. "We've talked about ideas like this several times, but we were never willing to risk placing something like this in any singular haven. However, there's a giant old building at the Protector Academy. They've been wondering what to do with it. My proposal is to create a haven within that building."

I flip to the next page as Evenia cocks her head to the side, eyes roving over the paper. "I've confirmed, from a security standpoint, this could work. Grand Portal Station haven would be surrounded by all the best protectors from our system—twenty-four hours a day of guards. Not to mention, we could easily create a failsafe to move the station haven into a prison cell if it's ever attacked. And since it would never be exposed to the human world, it would be at far less risk of being attacked by thralls or any of the monsters choosing to live in the human world."

Evenia points to the drawing of the building. "Talk to me about accessing this haven. How would that work?"

I've got her. Fuck. I think I've actually got her.

Forty minutes later, she sags against her desk, eyeing me with a surprised, thoughtful expression. "Gods above, Valentina," she murmurs. "This might actually work."

18
ALESSANDRO

"She did it," I bark, rising from my chair and tossing my book aside.

Pietro glances through the doorway from his spot on Valentina's tiny porch. He's been "people watching," which really means he's like a dog at the front door, waiting for its owner to return home.

He rises and comes through just as my comm watch lights up. Everything inside me curls and sparks into hot flames at seeing her name. Or maybe that's her stroking us through the bond.

When I direct the watch to answer her, her voice sounds small and far away.

"Bad news first," she says with a tinkly laugh. "Even though this was my only meeting today, my schedule is now full to the brim with follow-on meetings."

"What's the good news, darling?" Pietro leans into the watch. "We need to hear you say it."

"Nothing is final," she says cautiously, "but it looks good. Everything. Even Grand Portal Station."

Pietro slumps forward, bringing his forehead to my chest as

he grips my right biceps with his fingers. His muscles tremble, our bond filled with relief like I've never felt.

"Come home," he growls. "As soon as you're able to. Congratulations, amore."

Her voice goes husky. "I'll be home as soon as I can get out of these meetings. But we did it, mates. This is going to happen, and I have you to thank for it."

"Thank us with your mouth," I say on a laugh. "I'll keep Pietro occupied until you're able to return to us."

"Actually, there's a great little café called Grind around the corner from my place. You should check it out. They've got food and great drinks. Might give you some ideas."

Smiling at Pietro, I agree. When we end the call, he glances up from my chest area. Our bond is fraught with need.

"Do you need me?" My voice is ragged and rough. The sheer joy of Valentina's success is overwhelming. We won't be able to celebrate with her for hours.

Pietro brings his mouth to mine and sucks at my tongue. Biting the tip, he rocks his hips against mine. "I need you, and I want to see this coffee shop. Perhaps we can play there."

Knowing Valentina, it wouldn't surprise me if that was exactly what she had in mind.

"Done," I breathe into Pietro's lips. "Let us grab our coats and go."

We manage to leave her apartment with minimal fucking around. As we head outside, it jars me that the sky remains black, the quiet snow falling just like last night. I'm not sure I could entirely get used to a haven where it seems to be night all of the time.

I'm lost in thought as we walk up the block toward the location she gave us.

"That's a great fucking name," I mutter when Grind comes into view. Like everything in this haven, the sign is black and white, and the entrance is darkly elegant. Wooden flowers creep and crawl up the front of the café, over the door and back down the other side. They're roses, threaded through with thorns and tiny platters with black wooden coffee cups. It's an incredible installation, and Valentina was right... it gives me ideas for Higher Grounds.

Pietro grabs the door for me, and I sail through with a playful pinch to his side. He hisses but follows me in. Except I stop in the doorway, shocked at the scene within.

This isn't just a coffee shop, it's a vampiric coffee shop. It's sex and blood and coffee all mixed together.

The first thing I notice is the giant minotaur strapped to the wall with both hands behind his back. He's blindfolded and naked, his cock erect and bobbing in the air. Two vampire females take turns licking and sucking on him as he lows quietly into the room. Watching them pleasure him tightens my sack. A third woman steps to his muscular stomach and sinks her fangs in, slicing his skin. She drips his blood into her drink, then laps at it to close the wound.

But it's not just him. Farther back down a dark hallway on the left side of the ordering area, other monsters are strapped to the walls, surrounded by vampires enjoying their bodies and their blood.

"Oh my gods," Pietro mutters, reaching down, I presume, to adjust an erection that matches mine.

I give him a sultry look. "And our woman sent us here to tease us."

"Spanking later," he says, walking toward the countertop where there's shockingly not a line.

I follow, taking in the right-hand side of the coffee shop, which holds a dozen small tables with monsters working on computers, reading, writing in notebooks as they enjoy their drinks. But the drinks aren't like ours. Nearly every drink has sticks dangling from it with bits of meat and vegetables, shrimp and all sorts of add-ons. One lovely female drinks a frothy troll-whip-topped coffee with a stick speared through a jalapeño pepper.

"Definitely getting ideas," I say to myself as I join Pietro.

It takes us five full minutes of examining the menu to pick our drinks. I opt for the Crimson Scar Espresso, and Pietro picks a Blood Clot Latte.

"This is fabulous," he says as we find a seat. Ten minutes later, we're still admiring the darkly decadent shop when a barista calls our names.

As I take my drink from the barista, she hands me a needle attached to a short tube. She gestures toward the wall. "Any monster with a blue card above their head has consented to being drunk from by a male. Simply slip the needle into an available vein until your cup is filled." She smiles at me. "Just don't forget to close up the wound. Makes a terrible mess when we don't."

Thanking her, I eye the line of available options. The minotaur has no blue card, so he must not be interested in males. Farther toward the back there's a handsome dark elf with a square jaw. He's not blindfolded, and he looks my way with a smirk. A blue card above his head indicates it would be fine to drink from him.

Stalking past tables of chatting vampires, I pause beneath him to admire how handsome he is. Rough stubble lines his jaw, long white hair pulled into a messy bun. Pieces of it hang down around his ears. The sudden urge to grip that bun and use it like a handle hits me, and I clear my throat to mask a groan.

"Hello, vampire," the dark elf says with a wicked grin, his teeth gleaming white from behind inky black lips. "See something you like?"

"Yes," I breathe out. This is the best coffeehouse I've ever been to. My naughty mate has sent me to heaven with this recommendation. "I haven't been to Grind before, but I am absolutely enthralled."

"I get that a lot," he says in a smug tone. "Drink from me,

handsome. Or better yet, suck my cock while you drink from me."

"Do you have a preference in locations?" I smile at him as I wave the bloodletting needle.

"Anywhere you want to suck is fine," he says agreeably.

I laugh. This male is impetuous and sultry, two things I adore in a partner. I drag my nails down his thigh, watching his fat cock bounce against his leg. He grits his jaw, staring at me like he'd eat me alive if he could escape being tied to the wall.

"Locations for bloodletting?" I ask again as I inch closer, hovering my mouth over his dick, wondering what he might taste like.

"The closer to my cock the better," he answers, stretching against his bindings.

His sensual words are giving me ideas. Like how we should perhaps invite him home and enjoy him with our mate.

"Noted," I say with a wicked grin. His muscles tense and tighten, his cock bobbing to slap me on the cheek. Leaning down, I lap at the base of it, enjoying the way he grunts. I can feel his focus on me as he tries to rock his hips but can't.

Striking, I bury my fangs at the base of his dick and suck him down. He gasps and grunts and growls, nearly snapping one of the restraints. Once I get a good blood flow going, I press the bloodletting needle to the wound, watching as his dark red blood flows down the tube and into my latte. His scent mixed with the coffee has me ready to fuck.

I tap the edge of my cup as his blood fills it to the brim. Tucking the bloodletting tube under my arm, I lean forward and suck at the wound as he hisses. A quick lap of my tongue will clean the blood so the wound heals faster.

Black eyes flash at me, his interest obvious. He lifts his chin. "Our chemistry is obvious. Tell me you want to take this somewhere, because I want to take this somewhere."

"I'll ask my mates," I tease, straightening away from him. "How might I find you if they're interested?"

He jerks his head toward a small placard at his feet. "My info's there."

I glance at the sign.

"Diavolo, what a beautiful name." I lap at the edge of my cup, his eyes following the movement of my tongue.

"Call me," he commands, bristling the hair on my nape.

"I just might, Diavolo," I croon, turning from him. But I sense his focus on me all the way back to the table.

Pietro's eyes fall to my cup as I set it down. He leans over and grabs it, taking a slight sip. His second eyelid flashes over his eyes as he looks toward the dark elf bound to the wall behind me. He'll have heard the entire exchange, so I don't need to fill him in.

"Decadent," he says. "We should definitely call him. Valentina would enjoy that."

"Not just Valentina," I admit with a laugh. "We are definitely calling him."

Pietro's crimson eyes flicker to the male again. He sips his espresso with a smile.

Behind me, the dark elf's low rumbling is the perfect backdrop to a drink full of his delicious, sensual blood.

19
PIETRO

Three months later

Diavolo stands by my side on the training field at the Protector Academy in Hearth HQ. He wears an elegant charcoal-gray suit, long white hair pulled into a disheveled bun on top of his head. He leans in, brushing his lips along the edge of my ear as we stare at the giant renovated building the new Grand Portal Station haven was built inside of. "She looks fucking stunning, so full of joy and pride."

Alé joins us, handing us both a glass of champagne. "She's going to want us later." He rubs at his chest. "She's so hyped with excitement for today."

Nodding, I turn and nip at the dark elf hovering by my side. Turns out we *thoroughly* enjoyed him. So much so that we've invited him to join us on many occasions. I think he's Valentina's favorite plaything, and he adores being used by her.

Glancing around, I take in the huge crowd standing in front

of the former empty building. Now it's dark but shiny and new. A huge, elegant white-lettered sign announces it as Grand Portal Station. Rows of armed gargoyles and minotaurs stand in front of the building with Evenia, Valentina and her team.

A giant red ribbon is stretched across vaulted double doors into the new haven.

Evenia clears her throat into a microphone, and the gathered beings fall silent.

The haven system's original designer stands tall and haughty at the front of the crowd. "Welcome, monsterhood." Her voice is powerful, carrying a strength that belies just how ancient she is.

She opens her arms wide. "Welcome to Grand Portal Station. Monsters have long asked for an easier way to travel between havens. But safety came first, and we never had a good solution that would keep safety in mind. But—" she turns to Valentina, "—my Chief Haven Designer, Valentina, came up with a brilliant idea. The culmination of that idea is what we've invited you to see today."

I'm a little surprised at her kind words. Evenia's never been known for that. Alé, Valentina and I even joked this morning that Evenia would likely demand to cut the red ribbon.

I'm further surprised when Evenia drones on for a few minutes but hands a pair of giant scissors to Valentina. My mate's beautiful ruby eyes find us in the crowd, our bond full of love, pride, and shock.

"You've got this," I whisper, knowing she can feel my adoration through the bond.

Alé sends his wonder and awe of her along our connection, and I smile.

We're here. Finally. After centuries of painful longing, after centuries of never being able to sleep in the same bed for more than a few days at a time.

Valentina takes the scissors and turns to the carved black wood doors. Monsters of every species are represented. It's a beautiful testament to the new world this project opens up for us.

I hold my breath as she cuts the ribbon and it flutters down onto the ground. A gargoyle female steps forward and takes the scissors. Valentina grasps the door handles and pulls them wide, revealing a protective ward surface.

The crowd erupts into murmurs and whispers as she turns and smiles broadly at us. "Come on in, please!" With that, she turns and disappears through the portal's surface and into the building.

It takes a few minutes for the entire crowd to traverse the portal into the enormous, cavernous room on the other side.

"Holy fuck," Alé gasps out. "A million mockups couldn't do this justice."

I reach for his hand as I stare around the room. A glass ceiling above gives the impression of sunny, beautiful skies. I know from talking with Valentina that the sky's weather will change all the time. It'll be beautiful to be inside this building at sunset.

White stone walls are carved with frescos representing the havens that helped provide feedback for the portal station. All along the oval outline, green portal doors gleam and shine.

Evenia climbs on top of a small stage and grabs a microphone. "Welcome to Grand Portal Station! If you'd like to take a short trip to any other haven, they are all represented by the portals in this room. We encourage you to take a quick visit."

The room grows loud with excited monsters. Many disappear through portal doors with visible excitement. Between every portal door are small shops—cafés, restaurants, newsstands, gift shops, and more.

Valentina appears at my side and slips her hand through the crook of my elbow. "Wanna see it?"

Excitement fills me.

"Absolutely," I say on a growl. Tugging a smiling Alé with us, I follow my mate to the far end of Grand Portal Station. The far end isn't completely finished, but Evenia didn't want to delay the grand opening.

We pause in front of an unopened café. A sign at the top reads "Higher Grounds."

"It's beautiful," Diavolo whispers, having followed us.

Valentina beams at him, then looks at Alé and me. "I know you'll want to be here a lot as you get close to opening, but I wanted to show you how much progress we've made on your plans."

Evenia got strict the closer to opening day they got. Alé and I weren't even allowed to visit our second location for fear of something being leaked to the public. So, Valentina has been managing our build for the last few weeks.

"Want to see inside?" she asks, tickling Alé on the side.

"Hells yes," I bark out.

Laughing, she sashays behind a giant curtain that covers the front of the café. We follow, pushing and shoving to see who can get there first. Well, Diavolo trails Alé and me, always cautious not to intervene between us.

Inside, I halt, and Alé nearly stumbles over top of me. The interior is all black and gold, elegant beyond belief. A granite floor gleams with shiny stones, red rubies inlaid in trailing patterns over the surface. The walls are carved wood like the rest of the station, but they feature an elegant design that mimics vampiric house tattoos. The walls are painted dark, and, similar to Grind, there are spots to bind obliging monsters to the wall. We've put a unique spin on it though. The platforms can retreat up into the ceiling for more privacy.

"This is stunning," Diavolo whispers, walking around the space with his big arms held aloft. He gives Valentina a saucy look. "Come here and kiss me."

She laughs and crosses the floor, sinking easily into his arms as Alé and I exchange smirks.

We're going to christen the new location.

"We're not," Valentina barks as she separates herself from Diavolo. "I can feel what you're thinking, and we are absolutely not doing that today. But soon." She slaps Diavolo on the stomach. "Maybe we'll strap you to the wall and tease you."

"I am willing and ready." He reaches for her as she dances out of his grip.

Alé and I stride forward, pressing her against the dark elf as he beams. "Tease her," I command my mate.

Alé reaches down and slides his hand up her skirt, stroking as she moans and looks at us, eyes hooded with desire. "We really cannot do this right now," she manages, but pink travels across her cheeks as Diavolo starts licking soft circles down her neck.

"We can," he encourages, always ready to ignore the world in order to pleasure her.

She laughs and slips away from us and across the room.

We stand together and stare at her.

"You need to be chased," I growl, balling my fists.

She doesn't wait to see if I make good on that comment. Instead, she dives out of the space with a laugh and disappears into the main room. Our bond is flush with pleasure. I'm guessing she's got plenty to do today before we can take her home.

Diavolo presses his big body to Alé's back and slides both hands down the front of Alé's pants, stroking an obvious erection. "Let me do something about this," he offers.

Alé lets his head fall back against Diavolo's shoulder and reaches for me. "Yes," he murmurs. "Definitely do something about this so I don't have to go back out there with a raging hard-on."

Twenty minutes later, my mate has come twice, head lolling against Diavolo's shoulder as he groans softly. My hands are covered in sticky cum.

Diavolo purrs and spins Alé to face him, licking him clean. I watch, fascinated, as his dark gray tongue dips behind Alé's sack.

"Got to get home," Alé moans. "I can't take more of this. Grab Valentina, and let's go."

I watch until Diavolo's ministrations have Alé hardening again. Laughing, I flick the tip of his pointy ear. "Come on, let's find Valentina and see how much longer she needs to stay."

We manage to make it out of the coffee shop and find her, but it's clear she's going to be busy for a while. We venture all the way around Grand Portal Station, admiring every detail, details we've only been able to see on paper since so much of it came together in the last few weeks. Even after all of that, she's still surrounded by monsters who want to interview to her.

The crowds have begun to dissipate, but she'll be here a while.

We wait until there's a break in the crowd, then Alé paces to her side, rubbing her elbow.

She turns with a bright smile, rising to her tiptoes to kiss his lips. When she drops back down, he threads a hand through her hair. "We're going to head home, amore, so you can do this without worrying about us. You were marvelous today."

She beams and rubs both hands up his chest. "I'll be home as soon as this is done. You're going to use the Ever portal, right?"

I laugh, surprised. Traveling through the Grand Portal Station hadn't even occurred to me. "I'd forgotten," I admit.

"Give it a try." Ruby eyes flick to Diavolo. "I'd like you there, if you're free tonight." She laughs and gestures around us. "You can always come home tomorrow!"

Diavolo croons and slips a muscular arm around my waist, pulling me close. "I'd love to, darling. Pietro will have dinner on the stove when you get home, and I'll be teasing Alé to get him ready for your teeth."

"Perfect," she says breathlessly. She kisses each of us in turn, but when I open my mouth to say goodbye, someone grabs her and drags her to a group of monsters waiting to speak with her.

Alé, Diavolo and I turn and head for the Ever portal. It's at the far end near our new location.

"There's so much to do," Alé says as we come close to the portal. "Now that we're allowed back in, we need to figure out how to bring everything through, and—"

I grab his hand and thread my fingers through it. "And it'll be easy, because we can step right through the portal and go back and forth."

Alé's expression goes thoughtful as he stares at the green portal next to our new location. A beautifully hand-painted sign above the portal door reads "Ever." Looking up, I smile, because I hadn't noticed until now that security is placed all around the cavernous station.

A dark purple gargoyle crouches quietly on a small platform far above the door, near the ceiling. He barely moves. When I listen, there's no heartbeat.

So he's unmated.

Tipping my head to him, I follow Diavolo and Alé through the portal.

It's different from Ever's portal, which is a long green tube. This is more of a short hallway. We emerge on the opposite side, stepping into Shifter Hollow's portal station, which bustles with monsters I don't recognize.

That means tourists.

And tourists mean money.

All the sleepless nights, all the tears, it all feels worth it, knowing our beautiful mate will come home to us tonight. And tomorrow? Well, tomorrow she'll come right back here to work with a far shorter commute.

I push love through our bond, smiling when she shoves it right back like a hug for my soul.

Ahead, Diavolo and Alé rib each other as they walk toward the portal station's exit. And I smile watching them. We are so, so, so lucky.

20

VALENTINA

The fake sky above us shimmers every shade of pink and purple as it emulates a sunset. I sit on a bench in a gorgeous, modern seating area in the middle of the portal station, watching as monsters come and go. They seem to marvel at how easy it is. Two minotaur males holding hands emerge from the portal to Rainbow, in America's New York state. The smaller male cries quietly. Once they're out of the portal, the bigger one pulls him into his arms.

I don't mean to eavesdrop, but vampiric hearing is so good that I pick up their conversation. They haven't visited home in years because there used to be over forty portal stops between Hearth HQ and Rainbow. Now it's one portal. They just saw a friend for the first time in decades.

Smiling, I move my gaze around the room. How many families will be reunited because of this station? How many love stories—like mine—will have happier endings because of it? Tears fill my eyes until I hear the familiar clack of Evenia's signature heels. Brushing the tears away, I stand and smooth my jacket and skirt.

My boss stops next to me, hands clasped at her waist. She eyes me up and down, her gaze cool and assessing. Like always, I lift my chin and return her vicious smile.

To my surprise, her smile grows wider, seeming almost genuine. She looks around the portal station and sighs.

I don't dare say a word.

Eventually, she looks at me. "You did a good job, Valentina. You convinced me to do something that many monsters have tried to convince me of over the years. But I always found fault with their plan. Well done."

I'm almost too flabbergasted to respond, but I manage to thank her as gracefully as I can.

Her smile goes thoughtful. "You almost remind me of me, a little bit, when I was younger." She casts her eyes down my figure and back up. "I was more cutthroat. You're softer around the edges, but moldable, I think."

Gods, I hope she doesn't think that was a compliment?

She stares at the portal directly in front of us. It leads to Azuro, my home haven. "We're overwhelmed with applications for the first wave of monsters to move from Azuro to Tesoro. That's because of you, too. You've shown enormous creativity in the design of that haven. I can't wait to see what you come up with for the next one. Rainbow grows large; we should tackle another New York location next."

"Of course," I say as smoothly as I can. That she wants to start another project so soon speaks volumes about her confidence in Tesoro's success. We're not even done building it yet!

Evenia turns on her heel, glancing at me over her shoulder. "Don't let my praise go to your head, little dove. I'll be expecting more from you now that you're Chief Haven Designer. You'll be working many nights and weekends. Who knows if you'll even have time for those two pretty mates of yours."

That said, she stalks off toward the exit, leaving me in a cloud of ecstasy despite her parting commentary.

The work ahead of us will be time-consuming, but doing it

has always been my dream. Grinning, I grab my bag and head for the portal to Ever.

Time to go home.

A quarter hour later, I push through the front door of our apartment above Higher Grounds. The scent of blood calls me, Pietro and Alé teasing me through our bond. It's not their blood, though. No, it's my elf's.

Smiling, I toss my bag onto the counter and walk down the hall to the playroom. When I enter, I find Diavolo hung from the ceiling by a series of ropes, his cock dripping precum onto the floor as Alé laps fervently at his sack.

"Hello, boys," I greet them as I kick off my shoes.

Pietro rises from a chair and comes to me, pulling me into his arms for a kiss that steals my breath. When we part, he spins me to face Diavolo, whose face is scrunched up as he pants and cries out, begging for relief.

"You're home," he croaks. "Gods, please let me come. They said I could come when you got home."

Pietro moves to my back, piling my hair on top of my head. He brings his mouth to my neck and bites. Orgasm hits me, and I thrash in his arms, liquid heat soaking my panties as I come hard enough for my knees to buckle. My mate holds me steady, the rock keeping me safe and secure as bliss barrels through me.

"Please," Diavolo begs again. "Let me out of these ropes. I need you."

"Join me, mate," Alé offers before returning his focus to Diavolo's cock and balls.

"Let him down," I command. "I need a 'welcome home' kiss."

With a beleaguered sigh, Alé pulls a few bits of rope, releasing Diavolo carefully to the ground.

In moments, the dark elf is on his feet, crossing the short distance between us. He grips my throat and pushes me hard against Pietro, hovering his lips over mine with a soft snarl. "They've been torturing me for hours, Valentina. Hours."

I reach up and stroke my knuckles along his sharp jawline, eyes locked to his as he breathes hard, chest heaving.

"My poor, needy elf," I croon. "Do you need relief, my sweet?"

"Yes," he moans. "But I want to give you something first." He looks over his shoulder at Alé, then back at Pietro and me. "Something I've wanted to give you for a while."

He drops his grip on my throat and takes a few steps away from us as Alé joins Pietro and me.

My beautiful mate plants a kiss on my shoulder. "Welcome home, by the way."

I smile as we stand together, staring at Diavolo. The elf's expression is serious—more serious than I've ever seen it in the months we've known him.

"Dia, are you okay?" I start forward just as I hear the first crack of bone. Shocked at the loud noise, I rush to him.

He pulls my hands to his chest. His skin is scorching hot. Another crack rends the air, followed by another. Before my eyes, Diavolo's body grows. His arms, legs, and torso grow longer. His horns flex and thicken.

"My gods," Alé whispers.

"Are you sure?" I look into pitch-black eyes, and what I see there is something more than the playful relationship we've developed with the dark elf. I see commitment. I see desire. I see…adoration.

"I'm sure." He holds my hands on his body as he grows and grows until he's nearly ten feet tall. His beautiful black horns easily add another three or four feet to his height.

"I've never seen a dark elf in their true form," I whisper.

He smiles at me. "I've never shown anyone my true form. Not a single time in my entire life." He looks around as my mates join us. "But I wanted to show the three of you. I want you to drink from me like this."

Pietro gasps. "Are you sure, Diavolo? This is a gift beyond measure."

Dark elf blood is priceless, more valuable than gold and gems all together, due to its ability to strengthen any type of magic and heal any illness or wound. Thousands of years ago, they were hunted for that very reason. But some smart ancestor devised a way to bind their blood with magic. Now, its magical properties only work when the blood is freely given.

"I want to share this with you, all of you," he repeats. "It would be a great honor for you to drink from me."

"Of course, my sweet," I whisper, the first tear spilling down my cheek. "How would you like us to take you?"

He moans, reaching down to pull me up into his arms. His lips brush against mine. "Violently. Over and over. Take me any way you want to, Val."

I love his nickname for me. Both of my mates call me Valentina, and I love the way they say it. But with Diavolo, we're Val and Dia. It's different.

It feels right.

"Me first," I spit out, bloodlust rising at the idea of taking him. I've learned in a short time that Dia loves being attacked by us. The more violently we take him, the better for him. He loves to be chased, bitten, subdued, bound. Lifting my ziol necklace, I press the button on the back to release the blades. Moving quickly, I slash the ziol across his throat.

He grunts, eyes rolling into his head as crimson blood spills from the wound. The scent of his pure-form blood hits me like a truck, and I press my face closer to him just to smell it.

Fucking divine. His blood smells better than any blood I've ever smelled in my entire godsdamn life. Like berry and moonlight and glittering gems all rolled together. His scent bursts across my senses, igniting my need to drain him dry. The lust overtakes me, and I surge forward, lapping at his neck as he cries out, bringing a hand to the back of my head.

I barely notice as Dia begs Pietro and Alé to join us. But then they bite him, and his soft moans turn into deep, earthy growls that rumble his chest and force blood spurting from the wound, coating my mouth and tongue. I can't drink him down fast enough. Liquid moonlight flows down my throat, igniting me from the inside out as I drink and drink.

Somehow, we make it to the bed, Dia pulling us down on top of his enormous figure. Pietro and Alé join me, biting and sucking at his neck wound while our big elf moans and writhes beneath us.

I pause long enough to press my hand to the side of Dia's face. He turns immediately, kissing and licking at my palm, sucking my fingers into his mouth.

Heat flares through me, my predatory senses narrowing and homing on his beautiful lips. But I force that instinct down.

"Thank you for this gift, Dia," I whisper, rubbing his cheek until he halts his ministrations and looks at me.

"You're the only ones I ever want to show this to," he says quietly.

Pietro and Alé stop lapping at Dia's delicious blood, moving closer to me as we stare at the dark elf. Dia shifts onto his elbows, the wound at his throat still flowing freely. His blood calls me. But his need, his sincerity...they call me more.

"What is it, my sweet?" I press a hand over his heart, rubbing soft circles over his ebony skin.

Black eyes move between the three of us, midnight lashes fluttering against his cheeks as he seems to compose his thoughts.

"I want you to keep me," he says after long, quiet moments. "I want to enjoy this form with the three of you, and no one else. I...I want to be here all of the time."

The three of us.

That makes me think of Alé and Pietro and how it was always the three of us. How we knew it would always *be* the three of us.

Yet when I examine my heart and the bond I share with my

mates, they're both excited, almost relieved to hear Dia's words. They want him. We all want him.

"We want that too," Alé whispers, pressing forward to take Dia's lips in a passionate kiss.

A black tear streaks down my elf's face as Pietro moves in and steals a kiss, whispering something sweet into Dia's mouth.

And then he looks up at me, eyes full of adoration.

"I love you, Dia," I whisper.

"Good," he manages with a low growl. "Now come fuck me before my cock falls off from neglect."

Laughing, I wait for him to shift out of his pure form and back into a manageable size. Pietro and Alé guide me to Dia's lap, and then we obey his command over, and over, and over.

Mine. They're all mine. And I couldn't be happier.

THE END

BOOKS BY ANNA FURY (MY OTHER PEN NAME)

DARK FANTASY SHIFTER OMEGAVERSE

Temple Maze Series

NOIRE | JET | TENEBRIS

DYSTOPIAN OMEGAVERSE

Alpha Compound Series

THE ALPHA AWAKENS | WAKE UP, ALPHA | WIDE AWAKE | SLEEPWALK | AWAKE AT LAST

Northern Rejects Series

ROCK HARD REJECT | HEARTLESS HEATHEN | PRETTY LITTLE SINNER

Scan the QR code to access all my books, socials, current deals and more!

@annafuryauthor
liinks.co/annafuryauthor

ABOUT THE AUTHOR

Hazel Mack is the sweet alter-ego of Anna Fury, a North Carolina native fluent in snark and sarcasm, tiki decor, and an aficionado of phallic plants. Visit her on Instagram for a glimpse of the sexiest wiener wallpaper you've ever seen. #ifyouknowyouknow

She writes any time she has a free minute—walking the dog, in the shower, ON THE TOILET. The voices in her head wait for no one. When she's not furiously hen-pecking at her computer, she loves to hike and bike and get out in nature.

She currently lives in Raleigh, North Carolina, with her Mr. Right, a tiny tornado, and a lovely old dog. Hazel LOVES to connect with readers, so visit her on social or email her at author@annafury.com.